LORDS
OF
THE
UNDERWORLD

LORDS
OF
THE
UNDERWORLD

BEYOND
A CONTEMPORARY MYTHOS

CARLY SPADE

LORDS
OF
THE
UNDERWORLD

BEYOND A CONTEMPORARY MYTHOS

Copyright © 2023 by Carly Spade

WWW.CARLYSPADE.COM

Published in the United States by World Tree Publishing, LLC

This is a work of fiction. References to real people, events, establishments, organizations, or locales are intended only to provide authenticity, and are used fictitiously. All other characters, and all incidents and dialogue, are drawn from the author's imagination and are not to be construed as real.

Cover and Interior Formatting by We Got You Covered Book Design

WWW.WEGOTYOUCOVEREDBOOKDESIGN.COM

CONTENT WARNING:
Story contains mild violence, sexual content, and themes surrounding death.

1876
IN THE AMERICAN OLD WEST...

ONE
THANATOS

"WHISKEY?" NOW THERE WAS a voice that parted clouds for the sun. Clementine Nichols.

Lifting my chin, I slid my hat back, smiling at her, accentuating the enlarged canines that death gods could never fully disguise. And yet, she never batted an eyelash at them. "Clem. Now there's a sight for sore eyes. Didn't think you worked tonight, sweetheart."

I sat in my usual corner in the larger of several saloons established in town. I'd preferred the shadows with walls at my back. An opportunity to sit undisturbed and observe, keep watch, and above all else, maintain the imposing nature I'd grown synonymous with through the ages. Such is the personification of death himself. A rolled cigar hung from my lips, and serpent twirling tendrils of smoke collected in the air in front of me. I slid the black-brimmed hat far enough to conceal half of my face but not so far to impede my vision. Brown scuffed leather boots pressed against my shins as I shifted my feet and leaned back, draping an arm over the back of the rickety wooden chair.

Grinning, her green eyes sparkling, Clementine rested a tumbler of amber liquid before me. "I didn't think so either. But Missy ain't feeling well, so here I am." She curled the wooden tray against her chest, swaying her hips from side to side.

Mortal men of all varieties occupied surrounding tables—drinking, carousing, gambling with cards, and occasionally flipping a table when the game didn't go how they wanted. That's when the saloon girls would step in to calm the heat, and keep the men happy, drinking and spending money. Several men were positioned at every corner, ready with their six-shooters resting on their hips if the women couldn't resolve the situation. Freddy Six-Fingers, an elderly fellow with no teeth, a blind eye, and only six fingers, played the piano, two pairs of couples dancing, swaying and tripping over each other's feet to the lively music. After rubbing a knuckle under his thick dark mustache, the bartender slung a towel over one shoulder, leaning on the bar to fill an empty tumbler with whiskey.

"How are you, Clem?" I lifted the glass to my lips, sipping

it and squinting at her.

Death was a natural occurrence for all organic beings. And it never wrenched me, bothered me, or tore a hole in my heart like with Clementine. She never told me, but tuberculosis slowly settled into her system, destroying her. She'd die younger than she wanted, and there wasn't a damn thing I could do about it. Such a vibrant heart only to be darkened by a shoddy fate. But even *I* couldn't twist destiny.

She shrugged, the specks of freckles littering her cheeks pinching together as she scrunched her nose. "Can't complain."

"Clem." I scooted forward on the seat, holding out my palm, beckoning her to slip her hand into mine. She obliged, my tanned skin making her porcelain fingers iridescent against the table's flickering candlelight. "How are you, *really*?"

Her nostrils flared at my touch, not out of fear or recoil but affection and lust. "I've been—" She gulped and shoved the tray under her arm with her free hand, twirling some of her long chocolate hair around one finger. "I've been feeling a bit tired lately, but I'm fine. Really, I am."

Over the past year, she'd lost considerable weight, and dark circles began forming under her eyes to never really fade away. And in the past week, I spied her hiding a handkerchief she'd discreetly cough into.

"It's none of my business, but you've turned away every woman who's approached you the past few months. Aren't you—I don't know—" Clem trailed off, her cheeks turning several shades of crimson.

"Not everything is about sex," I candidly finished for her. "Besides. My sights have been focused elsewhere." Lightly pulling her toward me, bringing her knuckles to my lips, I pressed a light kiss there, eyeing the gold poppy flower charm necklace she had worn since we met. And I could still appreciate the irony behind it.

Clem sucked in a breath, her breasts swelling beneath her eggplant-colored corset dress, chest pulsing up and down. "Please, Than." She shied away, trying to pull her hand away, her gaze averting.

"What? Why say it like that, sweetheart, hm?" I coaxed her back to me, using my thumb to caress the inside of her wrist.

"You must have the memory of a damn goldfish, Than." A fluttery chuckle escaped her throat. "About six months ago? I tried to kiss you. You put your hand on my mouth and said quote, 'It wouldn't be fair.'"

Closing my eyes, I sighed—defeated and shattered. I'd been a fool to think she somehow would forget that. But I spoke the truth in far more ways than one. The most unfair bit? I knew she wasn't the one—my fated love. In some selfish bout of revenge, Hekate shared with me one subtle detail about her. If she so chose, the woman who would become my eternal would possess onyx eyes. It was little to go off and drove me mad for centuries. I'd never know when she was born, where she'd be, or how to find her. But—her eyes would remind me of a midnight starless sky. Not to mention the woman's fate would be that of a goddess if she so chose it, and Clementine's fate had already been sealed.

"It wouldn't." I squeezed her hand, letting go and leaning back. "As an example, take a look at what I am, what I do. That doesn't bother you?"

Her eyes roamed my long black hair, traveling my rolled-up shirt sleeves and lingering over the silver and black revolver hanging from my hip by its holster. "No. The way I see it? You take care of the varmint. You *ain't* it."

The Fates could be so unknowingly cruel. This woman was the fresh misted air after a rainstorm, the rainbow afterward, and the warmth that followed in a single breath.

"And the rumors about that other side of me. That doesn't bother you either?" I doused the cigar under my boot heel and rested my forearms on the table.

"What? You mean the black wings? Your face turning partially skeletal? All those crazy things?" She laughed, her shoulders bouncing. "A terrified person could imagine a lot of things. Or, maybe, it's magic."

"Insightful." A gooey smile graced my lips.

"Yeah. Sleight of hand. I can do a bit of magic myself." She lifted her chin.

"Oh?" Sitting back, I raised a brow and slid my hands across the table.

"Yeah." She glanced around the saloon, the patrons' numbers dwindling as the night wore on. "Bout time for a break anyhow. Wanna see?"

"Absolutely."

A hitch formed in her step as she turned to rest the tray on a vacant table, swiping a deck of playing cards into her hand. After shuffling through them, she removed three, slightly bending them down the center, and sat in front of me, swishing her dress's train behind her.

"Three cards. And all you need to do is tell me where the lead card is. Simple, right?" She sat with perfect posture, tiny crinkles forming at the corners of her eyes with her smile, those charming dimples making an appearance.

"Very simple. What's the lead card?" Interlocking my fingers, I leaned forward, inhaling her perfume—floral and vanilla.

She flipped one card around, displaying the ace of spades. "I've always been partial to this one."

Involuntarily, my eyes darkened, a devious smirk playing on my lips. "The death card. One I've always been fond of."

Clementine's pinky traced the dip between her pale breasts, her heartbeat like thunder in my ears. "Somehow—I knew that."

I bit a canine down on my bottom lip and removed my hat, resting it on the table and out of the way. Dragging a hand through my long hair, I drummed a random beat with my fingers, watching her.

She held two cards in one hand, displaying the ace of spades and queen of hearts in one hand, king of clubs in the other. "All you need to do is follow death and tell me where it is."

Right in front of you, sweetheart.

"Understood."

Clem slapped the cards to the table, shuffling them, quickly working one over the other, with the backs facing outward. "It's a fairly simple game, friend. With a simple outcome. So, all you need to do is tell me—where's your card?" She left all three on the table, resting one beside the other, and flattened her palms to the wood.

I caught her gaze with mine, edging my hand toward a card I knew was *not* the ace of spades. "Death is anything but simple, Clementine."

The game was, in fact, a sleight of hand, one she was particularly good at, but despite her skill, my godly intuition would allow me to know where the card lay each time she tried. Her confidence and excitement were far too infectious to squelch.

Tapping the left card, I bobbed my brows. "This one."

After making a tsking sound, she flipped it, revealing the king of clubs. "Oo. So close. Care to try again?"

Reaching across the table, I rested my hands atop hers,

scraping the calluses on my palms against her fragile skin. "I never meant to hurt you, Clem. I thought about you countless times. Always do."

She studied my face, her hands trembling beneath mine. "Then why would it be so unfair?"

"It's—" I set my jaw and fell back in my chair with a subdued growl, resting my hands on my thighs. "—complicated."

"Well, much like death, love, too, is complicated." She blinked at me, her thin brown eyebrows pinching together.

For the sake of us both, I remained silent, despite her words sounding well beyond her years.

"I wouldn't mind wings, you know," Clem started, smiling but not looking at me, keeping her eyes focused on shuffling the three cards. "There's something particularly angelic about them."

A pit carved into my stomach, and I rubbed the stubble on my chin. "I'm no angel, sweetheart."

Her gaze lifted to mine, wide-eyed and wondrous. "Then what would that make you? If you really did have wings? A demon?" She'd shoved the word from a hidden place in her throat, croaking it.

Shaking my head, I didn't bother to secure the black tendrils of hair that'd fallen over my gaze, masking the anguished pull in my stare. "No. Something else, Clem. Something *else*."

She had yet to close her eyes, lips parting as if to ask another question, a new fiery curiosity—belief—flashing in her gaze.

The swinging doors flew open at the entrance, thudding both doors against the frame with a booming echo. All conversations died, along with the laughter, the piano keys tittering to silence. A man in a bowler hat held a dirty middle-aged man wringing a dingy brown hat between his hands.

"Something that needs to be dealt with, gentlemen?" I asked, shifting my attention to the two men, but keeping a side-eye on Clementine.

Mr. Bowler snarled and pushed the other man toward me. "You bet your ass it do—" He stopped short, gulping at me before removing his hat and pressing it to his chest. "M'lord. He owes me a gambling debt and hasn't paid for months. *Months.* Keeps on high-tailing town like a coward." He spat on the floor at the accused's feet.

Clementine scrunched her nose at the new saliva stain on the ground.

Nodding, knowing this man had done a lot more than avoiding a gambling debt, I flicked my wrist behind me. "You know the drill. In the back."

Rising, I slipped the hat back to my head, catching Clem by the elbow as she turned away, serving tray in hand. She gulped and stared at me, her pulse quickening as I lowered my lips, hovering at her jawline. "We'll continue this later, Clem. I promise."

"I'm holding you to that, Than." She turned, making our noses brush. "For now, both our duties call, hm?"

I let some of my chilled breath flutter across her skin, eliciting a whimper she swallowed away before pulling out of my touch and moving to a beckoning table needing more drinks. Letting Clementine's cheery demeanor fill my heart for one last moment, I turned on a heel, a grim shadow looming over me in another instant.

Pushing open the door, I found Mr. Bowler beating the other man's face in, pausing with a red-soaked fist in mid-air when I entered.

"What the hell do you think you're doing? You brought him to me for a *reason*, did you not?" I roared my words, amplifying them with my power, and making the one hanging lamp rattle.

"I thought I'd—thought I'd warm him up for you." Mr. Bowler wound up like he was about to punch him one last time.

Porting, I appeared beside him, blocking the swing with my forearm. "Out. *Now*," I growled, flashing my skeletal form over my face long enough to make him question his own reality.

"Jesus Christ," Mr. Bowler screeched before scurrying from the room.

The accused's face, bloodied and bruised, peered up at me, smiling with a missing tooth that he spat to the floor. "Thanks for that. I—"

After tossing my hat aside, I loomed over him, conjuring the feather black wings bestowed on me by the primordial gods I hailed from. The lethal curved claws at the arches caught the flickers of lamp light, and petrification traveled over the man's face like an oil slick.

"Believe me when I say, you have nothing to be thankful for except that you're dealing with *me* and not The Boss." I leaned into his face, making no effort to disguise its macabre deathly variety—blackened bone, hollowed eyes, cracks leaking fire. "Mid-winter is coming, and you missed him by *days*."

The man dug his heels into the ground, making every effort to get away from me but too terrified to process the how of it. I pulled out all the stops because the man was good as condemned. The stench of murder reeked from his soul, and the smell infuriated me, catapulting my efforts.

"Who did you *kill*, William? Hm?" I flared the wings, curling them around us, imprisoning him.

"Nobody. No one—how would you know if I—" He turned his gaze away, still whimpering.

Snatching his face in one skeletal hand, I forced him to look at me, death settling into his jaw, and the back of his skull. "Who do you think you're dealing with, human? I—am death incarnate. You weren't due to leave this existence for several days, but I say—no time like the present."

The man's eyes rolled back into his head, limbs convulsing as his body decayed and withered away piece by piece. I'd kept my touch from traveling to his vital organs, making him experience death as it overtook him—the pain and vulnerability of not being able to do a damn thing about it, just like the human he'd *stabbed* to death.

Once my touch reached his heart, slowly stopping its lively thrum, he disappeared in a heap of bones turned to embers and ash. His soul would travel to Styx, arriving on its banks for Hades to deal with now, my part of it done.

I stood for a long moment, allowing my nerves to settle, the will to disguise my godly form returning as I dug deep for the humanized version of myself. Envisioning Clementine's smile always helped when I lost myself in a frenzy. Once I assured myself the wings, the skeleton, that *death* would behave and keep hidden, I fitted the hat back on, flicking dirt from its brim. Back in the saloon, the man with the bowler hat stood waiting, perking up once he saw me. I dropped a rolled-up stack of money I'd conjured into his palms.

"I—" The man started, staring slack-jawed at the wad of cash I'd given him. "I feel I owe you a cut for getting this?"

Walking past him, not meeting his gaze, I shook my head. "I don't need your money."

"What about Bill? He still back there?" The man asked behind me.

"Don't worry about him. He's taken care of," I answered, cutting my gaze to Clementine and tipping my hat to her before slamming my palms into the swinging saloon doors.

Soon Hades would arrive, and it was time to prepare the town for it—to *remind* them.

Because mortal religious beliefs had, too, evolved. But it wasn't as if the Underworld gods were ever necessarily "worshiped" in the sense that Aphrodite or Athena was. Humankind has always feared us because the concept of death terrorized them. And in the nineteenth century, we used this fear to walk amongst them, to do something with our universally given gifts other than dwell in our caves.

We'd become enforcers, the locals lovingly labeling us "Lords of the Underworld." We'd take care of any problem the citizens had, whether it be large or small. Some issues were as trivial as a marital dispute, while others delved into murderous territory. Immortality, ancient power, and a sinister disposition lay in our arsenal. Considering we'd both witnessed the worst of the worst as far as humankind was concerned, little fazed us—and these folks *knew* it. Most of them. Those that remained unaware learned *quickly*.

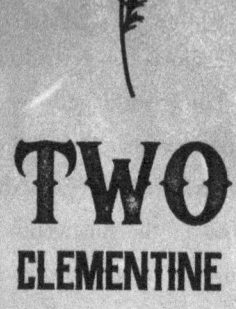

TWO
CLEMENTINE

DEATH HAD ALWAYS FRIGHTENED me—the mystery of not knowing what awaited for you afterward, no matter how hard you believed in something. The thought of my life simply coming to an end. That was it? Would I even know I *was* dead? But how things changed after a doctor told me my days on Earth would close sooner than I ever imagined. Tuberculosis. A sickness they could neither cure nor slow down. Time became both my savior and my enemy.

The saving grace? It gave me a new outlook on the world around me—things I never took the time to appreciate for what they were. Every sunny day seemed that much brighter, the thunder during a rainstorm gave me that much more of a thrill, even the buzzing of flies being flicked by a horse's tail made me smile. It also surged an extra ounce of courage through me, the desire to pursue something I'd longed for years prior. Time with one of two mysterious enforcers who threw our town off its axis the day they'd arrived. The one with long black hair that went simply by "Than" and the other with the ash blonde hair and light beard told us to call him "The Boss." And Than spoke to my very bones the moment our eyes met.

Visitors came and went in our town like passing trends. When they'd first shown up, most thought them nothing more than another couple of gunslingers looking for a duel or starting trouble in the saloon after too many whiskeys. So, when they announced they wanted to offer their services to help tame the town of low-lives, criminals, and degenerates? Well, that done colored us *all* surprised. The Boss would only stay a week out of the year, with Than coming and going as he pleased. But rumors started spreading about their intimidation techniques. The magic illusion tricks that made them look like they had wings or could conjure fire from thin air. I'd even heard one guy say something about Than's hands and face turning into a skeleton only to return to tanned flesh seconds later.

They killed folks when necessary—punished others for more minor deeds. Considering the rumors and the knowledge of what they did, Than should've frightened me, or at the very least, it should've made me keep my distance. Should. Have. But it didn't. The draw I felt toward him was like a prized pig to mud, and I couldn't ignore it. We became good friends through the years, but it never went beyond that. He'd occasionally visit the brothel, but lately, he went less and less. It'd been months since I last saw him shuffling into one of their rooms with a scowl.

I'd seen the way he looked at me. And I may not have had many lovers in my time, but a woman knew when a man showed interest. He liked me. I couldn't be sure whether it was my looks, personality, or both, but a spark *was* there. And that's why I took a chance. Live or die in the most literal sense. I went in for the kiss—and got denied. He told me, "It wouldn't be fair." Whatever the Sam Hill that meant, but I wasn't about to pry. And so, I made it my mission to get the answer I longed for *without* asking.

Stuffing the white handkerchief into a side pocket I'd sewn into my dress for just such a purpose, I padded my palms against my hair, eyeing myself in the dingy mirror of my rickety wooden vanity. After applying a bit of pink rouge to my cheeks and smoothing on red lipstick, I puckered at my reflection. The gold poppy flower charm hanging from its gold chain caught the flickering candlelight, and I ran my fingertips over it before turning for the exit.

In the early hours of the day, I went shopping for supplies, seeing as the only saloon-goers were the old timer regulars who spent nearly every penny to their name staying inebriated from dawn till dusk.

"I'll be back in a jiff, Fred," I said to the bartender, waving at him and holding my skirts as I passed through the double swinging doors leading outside.

Conveniently located across the street from the saloon, Tom's General Store stocked everything the town needed regarding farming, food, and other necessities. And if he didn't have it, he'd put in an order, and you'd have it within a month so long as the outlaws didn't rob the wagon on its way into town. But since the enforcers began their posts, stealing from the merchandise wagons became increasingly difficult. Knowing the new dress I'd ordered would be waiting for me behind the counter, wrapped in brown paper with a twine string, put an extra giddy-up in my step. And Than was partially to thank for that.

Tom lifted his head when the small bell above the door chimed. He offered a warm smile, adjusting the wire-rimmed glasses resting at the tip of his nose. I returned the grin and dug a hand into my coin purse, producing a handful of gold and silver coins.

"Afternoon, Clementine. Gather you're here for that parcel?" Tom's smile hadn't faded.

My grin widened, the ringlets of my brown hair bouncing

over my shoulders as I did a little hop. "It made it, then?"

"Sure did. That black-haired one with the never-ending scowl delivered it himself." Tom pointed a gnarled finger at me, removing the packaged dress from storage beneath the counter and resting it in front of me.

My cheeks flushed, followed by my chest. Than made sure the dress made it from the wagon to the store. He probably thought I'd never find out he did it.

"Thanks, Tom. I'll also need a new set of rags and three tumblers for the saloon if you have them in stock?"

"Yes, ma'am. Gimme a sec to get the tumblers. Keep 'em in back so they're less likely to get broken." Tom coughed and spat chewing tobacco into a spittoon in the corner as he passed it.

Smiling at the package, knowing the purple dress rested unscathed inside, I dragged my fingertips over the wrapping and sighed. It'd become a rare luxury having the money to afford a new dress, and every time I was able, it felt akin to swimming through the stars.

"Here we are," Tom said, clearing his throat and resting the rags next to my packaged dress. He ripped three pieces of brown paper and continued to pad each tumbler.

"Great. Thank you. How much do I owe ya?" I jiggled the coins in my hand, waiting.

Tom scratched his bald head. "Ten dollars should about

cover it, I figure."

"For—for everything?" I blinked, taken aback.

Tom snorted a laugh and one-shoulder shrugged. "Want me to charge ya more?"

"No," I yelped. "I mean, ten dollars sounds entirely fair. Thank you." Counting out the coins, I rested them in Tom's open palm and scooped the parcels into my arms.

"Clementine, you feeling alright?" Tom peered at me over the rim of his glasses, the till dinging open, and he dropped the coins into their appropriate slots. "You been looking a bit more tired lately."

My throat tightened, fighting back the urge to cough, and forced a grin. "Right as rain, Tom. Thanks again."

Exiting the store, I pinched my lips to hold back the cough, but it forced its way out. The familiar copper taste speckled my throat, some escaping my mouth and collecting on my lips. Grimacing, I reached for the handkerchief in my pocket, dropping the packaged dress.

Before it hit the ground, a pair of bronzed hands caught it, preventing it from landing in a muddy puddle. A cowboy knelt before me and stood tall, holding the parcel out to me with a sparkling grin. "Miss? I believe you almost dropped this?" Still smiling, he held it to me, tipping his cream-brimmed hat with a free hand.

Chip Dalton. I recognized him immediately. The most

sought-after cowboy and horse tamer this side of the Sacramento River.

"Thanks so much. Haven't even had the chance to get the wrinkles out of this thing yet. Would've been ruined." I clutched the parcel to my chest, offering him a smile.

Chip squinted against the sun, pointing at me. "Wait. Clementine, right? You work at the saloon?"

"That's right."

He slapped his thigh and grinned wider. "Well, you're just lookin' prettier than a snow-white mare."

Scrunching my nose, I scratched the back of my head. "Thanks. I think?"

"It's a compliment. Trust me." He edged the hat away from his forehead, wiping sweat with his jacket sleeve.

"On account of the horse taming and all?"

Chip chuckled, securing the hat to its rightful position. "Guess my reputation precedes me, hm?"

"At least it's a good one." The skin at the back of my neck heated due to standing in one place with my pale skin exposed to the blazing sun.

"Right, you are, Clementine. Right, you are." Chip flicked a piece of wheat stem at the ground, smiling at me and squinting.

"If you ever fancy taking a break in the saloon, I'll spot you a drink." I adjusted the items in my arms, ensuring none would fall again.

"Thank you kindly, miss. I'd appreciate that." He gave a curt nod, tipping his hat again, and I moved past him, not glancing at him.

When I entered the saloon, Freddy's piano playing bounced gleefully off the walls with no bodies to mute the sound. Humming to myself, I whisked to the bar, handing the bartender Teddy the items I'd purchased. He took them with a gentle smile and gave me a quick peck on the cheek. Tapping my feet to Freddy's jovial song, I moved to the piano, leaning on its side with a wistful sigh.

"Howdy, Clementine. How you doing today?" Freddy didn't stop playing and bobbed his head, keeping the same rhythm.

I smoothed out the skirts of my dress. "Can't complain. You wouldn't happen to know any flamenco music, would you? That dance they do in Spain?"

Freddy paused and raised a bushy brow at me. "Can't say I know anything about no flaming cow music. How'd you hear it if it's outta Spain, anyhow?"

"It's *flamenco*, Freddy," I corrected, giggling. "And I haven't heard it. I'd love to, though. I've seen paintings of the radiant dresses they wear, the poses. I imagine the music has to be just as vibrant and sensual." Biting my lip, I twirled one ringlet of my hair, dazing into dreams of dancing in Spain—dancing anywhere else but America. Doubt I'd ever get to see anywhere else except for California. Wasn't so bad. We *did* have beautiful scenery here.

"You know, word on the tracks is a fellah creating some kinda contraption that'll let you listen to things without having to *be* there." Freddy folded his arms and leaned on his backless stool. When he closed his eyes, he started toppling backward, and I grabbed his shoulder with a cinched brow.

"Without being there? How's that work?"

"Beats me. But mark my words. I bet we'll see one in Tom's store within the year. I'm sure it'll cost an arm and a leg, but can you imagine it?" Freddy cackled and shook his head.

Music. Anytime? Anywhere? Sounded like heaven.

"In the meantime, lemme play you something toe-tapping and sultry-like." Freddy interlaced and cracked his six fingers before playing them on the keys.

I had to bite my cheek to keep from laughing as the familiar melody to "Get Along, Little Doggies" resonated from the piano, Freddy's singing soon following.

Patting his shoulder, I kissed the side of his head like one would their grandfather. "You're right. This music is *all* I need, Freddy."

And this place. Its people. A gal should feel so lucky to have called it all home.

Despite Freddy still playing, the sound faded from my ears as the doors swung open, a dark figure entering with his head held low, the gray-brimmed hat hiding most of his face save for the stubbled tanned chin.

Than.

My heartbeat throttled into a gallop, like it had every time that man walked into the saloon. It was like watching a moving painting. Shadows seemed to follow him from outside, darkening his demeanor, and dozens of scattered whispers seemed to float around him despite only one patron sitting at the bar. And the way he moved—no wide gait, no hitch in his giddy-up like most of the cowboys in town—he took one step after another like gliding across a frozen pond.

I never approached him immediately because he'd walk in quietly and stoically, always making a beeline for the same table in the corner. It was as if he needed to shake off the night he'd had, wherever he went when he wasn't in the saloon. And today, like every day, he sat with his back to the wall, giving him a panoramic view of the establishment. He kept his hat on for now and sat, lit a cigar, and waited. And he would stay there all day, unmoving, unless trouble stirred or someone waltzed in with a problem needing fixing.

I'd let several hours pass, watching him, studying him, making up countless stories in my head about his story, thinking maybe today would be the day I'd have the guts to ask him. But today *wouldn't* be that day. Instead, I held a finger up to the bartender, asking for a tumbler of two fingers deep whiskey, and stood still with it resting on my tray for way longer than necessary. A couple of the prostitutes from the brothel next door had their paws all over him, but he made no move to touch them back. I was too far away to make out the conversation but considering how the one woman sneered at him, he obviously sent them packing. And he'd been doing that more and more lately. Was it so wrong to get that hopeful flutter in my stomach? Maybe he did it because of—me?

"Clementine," Freddy's voice beckoned, making me yelp.

Gripping the edges of the tray, I shot my gaze to the piano player. "Hm. Yes?"

"You better go take that boy his whiskey before you drool in it." Freddy chuckled, his shoulders bouncing.

With as much subtlety as I could muster, I dragged a knuckle under my lip, reassuring myself that I didn't have drool collecting there. After giving Freddy a reassuring smile, I weaved through the now busy tables, avoiding random elbows and flailing hands from several men playing cards.

I approached from the side, taking a deep breath so my voice didn't appear shaky. I lifted my chin after pushing the tray against my hip to steady it. "Whiskey?"

And when those smoky quartz eyes lifted to meet mine, my very spirit shivered along with my quaking knees. His gaze always made me feel like the world's best-kept secret—and every time we were around each other came those same jitters as the first. Power and ravishment within one flick of his dark eyelashes. And when his lips parted to speak, I became his on the very first syllable.

THREE
HADES

SPRING ETERNAL WRITHED ON top of me, my fingers digging into her hips. Her bronzed skin from the agreed time spent above ground had faded back to its pearlescent sheen, the sun-kissed scent long since disappeared. Her wheat-colored hair hung in long tendrils, splaying her shoulders, and her breasts, and she bunched it in her hands as she rubbed herself against my stomach. I bucked my hips, meeting her thrust for thrust, skull pressing to one of several black satin pillows adorning my kingly bed.

She clenched around me, coming undone and crying out. My spine seized as I followed, a gritty snarl bubbling at the back of my throat. Jerking through my release, I let myself go boneless, sighing as she pulled herself away, flopping to her back beside me.

Moments like these, easing the other's tension through sexual acts, were some of the rarer intimate moments Persephone and I had shared as of late. We'd dine in silence, read separate books in the same room but never speak, and then the time of day would come to head to our opposing realms—mine seated on my throne near the banks of Styx, hers in the Elysian Fields.

It hadn't always been like this. What started as a selfish act on my part, aided by my brother Zeus to bring her to the Underworld, to make her *mine*, blossomed into genuine care for each other. Despite my warnings, she'd eaten the pomegranate seeds, and tied herself to this place—*doomed* herself to it. I never wished that for her, and it tore a hole in my heart. It was that moment I'd sworn to do everything in my power to ensure her happiness. I'd have given her the universe if I possessed the power. But over time, she changed, I changed, and the fondness dwindled into a sort of mutual tolerance.

She spent half the year above ground and the latter half in the Underworld, ruling with me per the deal stipulated by the King of the Gods. During our best years, I ached whenever she left because it felt akin to a sliver of my soul missing when she was gone. She told me she'd felt the same, even cried a time or two when it was time to go, claiming she wanted to stay below, with me, instead. But moments like those came fewer and thinner as the years went by and now, I couldn't remember the last time either of us had said, "I'll miss you."

Persephone sat up, combing her hair with pale fingers, and eyeing me over one shoulder. "I should get back to the Fields. I left some of them waiting too long as it is."

"They've been waiting their entire lives. What's a few more hours?" I slipped my hand behind my head, scratching the scattered hair on my chin, remaining in the mortal form she'd always asked me to stay in when we lay together.

"Hades," she whispered, lifting a knee to rest her leg on the bed, turning partially to face me, hands dropping to her lap.

I let my gaze fall to her bare breasts, nipples flushed with pink, before lazily bringing my eyes back to her face. A wrinkle formed between her brow, lips pursed. "Go, if you must. I have to feed Cerberus anyway, or he'll whine so loudly the cave walls will start pebbling."

She nodded, rising and swirling a hand around herself, producing a shimmering pink dress in a plume of flowers and sunlight. "I'll see you later tonight." She turned away, trailing her hands over the dress' bodice.

"Seph," I beckoned, waiting for her to look at me before continuing. "Tomorrow is mid-winter."

The months she stayed in the Underworld had grown increasingly difficult to get along, and in the last two years,

Thanatos and I had begun "enforcing" in an American town where the wicked patrons outnumbered the righteous tenfold. They'd known me only as "The Boss" and feared the one week I'd return to handle business. Persephone agreed to take both the Fields and Tartarus while I was gone for the week—a role she had become increasingly good with and *craved*. Oh, how we both changed.

"I remember," she said, her voice soft as petals in the spring wind. "I planned to give this to you tomorrow, but now that you brought it up…" She moved in front of me, holding out a glossy black box.

Sitting up with a quirked brow, I took the parcel, resting it on the bed between us. After removing the intricately placed blood-red ribbon, I opened the box to reveal a twin pair of black six-shooters with shiny metallic gold hilts. Lifting one, snapping it to the side to pop out the barrel, I ran my palm over it, making it spin. Engraved on the hilt were symbols synonymous with me, a serpent, cypress tree, skull, and—pomegranate.

"These are gorgeous, Seph. Thank you." I rested the revolver back in the box and gazed at her.

"You're welcome. Have fun on the surface, my King." She bowed her head, turning away again without a second glance.

"Persephone," I called out.

She rolled her bottom lip between her teeth, tilting her chin over her shoulder at me.

"Behave while I'm gone?"

A devious glint formed in her eye, a smirk playing at her lips. "No promises." And before she ported to the Fields, she gave a final gift—a small smile.

My entrances to the surface as "The Boss" were always a spectacle—and I reveled in it. With most of the Greek gods, *fear* bordered on the same ecstasy as one felt to be cherished by another, which helped with the dwindling love from my wife. And these townspeople leaked it in droves; the bitter stench weighed heavy in the surrounding air, and it fueled every step I took in my black boots, silver spurs sounding against the dirt road.

Squinting against the dirt collecting in the wind, I lit a rolled cigarette, puffing on it several times before throwing the spent match to the ground. The black-brimmed hat felt snug around my skull, the weight of the matching new pistols Persephone had given me comforting me, the holsters lightly bouncing against my outer thigh with each stride. Townspeople gathered in groups outside shops, the bank, and the saloon, gasping and pulling at each other's sleeves when they noticed me. A cloud passed overhead in the otherwise vibrant blue sky, blotting out the sun and creating devious shadows around me. I'd have loved to take the credit for the ominous effect but I had no power over the skies, let alone the weather.

California in an age of hog-tying, cowboys, saloons, and gunslinging. And Greece, my former home away from home, had evolved from its ancient times. Overtaken by Rome, only to gain their freedom from the Ottoman Empire in the current century, and now in a perpetual state of poverty. But then so was the state with most of the world. Though I didn't possess sooth-saying abilities, something told me things would get worse before better. Which made our roles hidden amongst them that much more vital.

A horse's hooves clicked and clacked as it passed before me, trailing a stagecoach behind it. The driver narrowly missed launching into a nearby pole from staring at me. I never fully released the ember wings in daylight amidst the town center. Still, every so often I'd conjure some of the burnt feathers and floating embers blazing with orange to flutter around me like an animated cape. Church bells sounded, and a group of children were the first people to clamor out of the building. One bumped into me, gasping and staring wide-eyed, her bottom lip trembling.

"Good day to you, 'lil miss," I said, tipping my hat at the small girl with braided auburn pigtails.

She gulped and played with her fingers, backpedaling and

tripping over a stone. "How—howdy, sir."

"Oh, dear heavens," a woman's voice whispered. "Luanne, get over here."

The child ran to her mother, the woman nodding at me but terrified all the same. A shop's bell chimed nearby, a man leaning on a lamp post drinking something from a brown paper bag.

"Boss," he said to me, nodding and holding the disguised bottle in a toast. "Suppose this means my weeks' vacation starts today, hm?"

"Suppose it does, Sheriff," I leaned on the same pole, flicking part of my black jacket over my hip to rest a hand on one revolver. "Been loud around here lately?"

An older man in a dirty pair of light blue long johns and boots strolled past us, whistling to the tune of *Red River Valley*. He had scarcely any hair to speak of atop his head and obvious cataracts settling in his vision, but the positivity he exuded had me reeling.

"Not much different than any other time. Gambling debts, drunken tomfoolery, two goddamned idiots dueling in the streets like they think they're Billy the damn Kid or some shit and shooting each other dead." The Sheriff spat tobacco to the ground, shaking his head and folding his arms.

I took a long drag from the cigarette hanging from my lips, controlling the smoke curling from it to hover around me before the wind took it away. "Well, I—" I started, but the faint sound of a hammer cocking echoed in my ears.

Using one hand to shove the Sheriff's head down, I whisked one pistol from its holster, firing a shot over his shoulder. The bullet landed dead center into an outlaw's forehead, his face half covered by a red paisley bandana, a sack of money cradled in his arm. His body fell lifeless to the ground, the hand holding the revolver going limp. Twenty-dollar bills breezed through the air, the townspeople shrieking as they took to the streets, nabbing what they could before the bank could retrieve it.

The Sheriff stood straight, holding a hand over his left ear. "I might be damn well deaf after that, but thanks all the same."

Smoke billowed from the pistol's barrel, and I twirled the gun once by its trigger before securing it home in its black leather holster. Kneeling by the body, I touched a finger near the bullet hole I'd left. "We'll finish this later." Starting at his boots, he disappeared as ash and embers. Only the bag of money and a blood stain in the dirt remained.

The Sheriff's jaw dropped, his eyes blinking, knuckles rubbing against them to take a better look. The townspeople were too busy scurrying around catching money to have paid my stunt any mind. And the Sheriff, per usual, was beyond intoxicated.

"You seen Than lately?" I dusted off my hands.

The Sheriff continued to stare at the vacant spot on the ground. "Same place that boy always is."

A tiny smirk creased the corner of my lips. Than was far from a boy. After pulling on my hat, leaving the Sheriff to contemplate what he'd seen, I headed for the saloon.

After pushing on the twin swinging wooden doors, I snapped my jacket collar, adjusting it and securing the black bandana further into my leather vest. The place had been bustling and full of activity before I walked in—all conversations ceased, poker chips clanked against tables, and bottles fell to the floor, breaking. But worst of all? The piano music stopped.

Removing another rolled cigarette from my jacket pocket, I moved to the piano, striking a match against the side of it, eyeing the player's four missing fingers. Leaning against the instrument, I took a long cigarette drag, blowing ringlets into the air above us.

"Don't stop playing on my account, good sir," I pointed at the keys with the lit cigarette and bounced my brow at him. "And make it something lively, would ya?"

Fire flashed in my eyes long enough for him to catch it, but ponder if it were the candlelight reflections—it wasn't. He jolted to attention, spine zipping straight, and he beefed it up by playing *Magnetic Rag*.

I bobbed my head to the beat, narrowing my eyes as I scanned the tables, taking several puffs of the cigarette until I found him brooding in his usual darkened corner. Clementine hovered near him, smiling and twisting her hair.

That love-sick fool. Emphasis on *fool*.

Weaving through the tables, I sidled next to Clementine, saluting the brim of my hat at Thanatos. "Brother. Hope I'm not interrupting anything?" I jutted my head at the brunette beside me, flashing my eyes at Than.

Thanatos glared at me, his black eyes carving daggers into my skull.

"Not at all, Boss." Clementine smiled and bowed her head at Than. "I'll let you two be."

I waited—*waited* for Thanatos to stop her, to encourage her to stay with us, but as usual he didn't say a damn word.

Catching Clem by the crook of the arm, I dipped my mouth to her ear, keeping my focus on Thanatos. "Why don't you stay, darlin'? Have a drink with us. Than happens to enjoy your company. Told me himself."

Thanatos had been leaning back in his seat and sat up, digging his nails into the table.

"Oh, I don't know. I should probably get back to work, but—" Clem started, pointing at the bar and scratching her head.

"It'll be fine. I know the owner." There was no hiding the wicked grin pulling at my lips now.

Me. I bought the place last year for our business use.

Thanatos made a steady beat against the table with his

forefinger, cracking it on the fourth tap and glaring my life away.

"Let me just freshen these gentlemen's drinks over here, and I'll be back in two shakes of a rattlesnake's tail." Clementine squeezed Thanatos's shoulder, relaxing him before she whisked away.

Grinning, I slid the black hat from my head and hung it off one chair. Before taking a seat, I raked a hand through my hair. "Thanatos. How you been?"

"You pull that deal, brother, and then you resort to small talk?" Thanatos shook his head, scooping the whisky tumbler in his hand and draining the rest.

"Somebody's gotta pull it, or you'd be lonelier than I am." Snorting a laugh, I leaned back in the chair and propped a boot on the table.

Watching Clementine across the room, Thanatos plucked one of several throwing knives he kept on his belt and flipped it between his fingers. "And I should be taking romance advice from *you* for what reason again?"

"Ouch." I leaned back in my chair, slapping a hand over my heart like I'd been shot in the chest. "Damn, truth hurts, don't it?" Chuckling, I let the chair settle back onto the wooden floor.

"It *is* good to see you, brother. Even if you're a giant pain in my ass," Thanatos grumbled, scratching his stubble with the blunt side of one knife.

"She doesn't have to be a goddess, you know," I cut my gaze

to Clem and raised a brow at him.

Mortals whose fates interwoven with ours could be turned into gods and goddesses with blessings from the three king brothers. Unfortunately, Clementine's fate was sealed, and it wasn't a fate that'd bring her to Thanatos's side for all eternity. But she, as well as my gloomy friend, deserved happiness, even if temporary.

"It has nothing to do with that, and you know it. You know her time is running out, Hades. Don't give me that." Thanatos's lip bounced in a snarl, and he dropped his face in his hands.

I leaned forward and slammed my fist on the table near him. "She has weeks, possibly *days*, Than. And she's taken an interest in you. Why not spend time with her? Because the only selfish bit I'm seeing, and I know that's what your excuse is, is that *you* won't have her forever."

He lowered his palms, anguish and longing playing in his gaze. "I can't tell her that I know."

"Why not?" I shrugged.

"Why—" Thanatos flailed his arms. "Why *not*? We play these charades with our true selves because we can work it as an intimidation technique. To tell her would be revealing who I am. Who *we* are."

"Do you think I give a shit about her knowing I'm the King of the Underworld?" Fire blazed in my eyes as I slid back, leaning in my chair again. "Tell her. Be with her. Give her happiness in the time she has left, Than, or it will eat you alive for a millennium."

He ground his teeth together, making his jaw tighten and flex. One hand curled into a fist on the table, he was clearly ready to give me a piece of his mind. Until Clementine returned, melting all aggravation into a lava puddle beneath the table.

"Here, Boss. I brought you a whiskey," Clementine chimed, her voice lilting and melodic.

"You're an angel, Clem. A living, breathing angel." I smiled at her, taking the glass into my grip and toasting her with it before sipping.

A fluttery laugh floated from her chest before she rested the tray on the table and sat beside Thanatos. "What I wouldn't give for a pair of wings. Imagine how fast you could get places. Faster than a horse any day, I'd figure."

"Imagine the possibilities," I added, grinning like a jackal at Thanatos over the rim of my tumbler.

A woman screamed from the road outside, and a man flew into the swinging doors from someone throwing him into the saloon. Thanatos and I pushed to our feet simultaneously, our hands launching to the weapons poised at our hips.

Another man, hulking and menacing, wearing only pants with suspenders and boots, entered next, snapping the suspenders against his bare chest. "You screwed up big this time, Hoss."

A blonde woman, her massive breasts bulging from the top of a scarlet red corset dress, followed soon after, pointing at the man groaning on the floor. "That man tried to fuck me without paying me. Tried to force me into a room to do it too," the woman shrieked as she held the tattered dress straps from exposing her.

Fury spiraled up my spine, and I moved to the man on the floor, taking a knee and forcing him to look at me. I played an inferno in my gaze, burning him with it once our eyes met. "Is she implying what I think she's implying, *bub*?"

"No, no, she's lying. I paid her, and the damn bitch tried to get out of it," the man stammered, his voice shaky as a trotting horse.

I first lifted my gaze to the woman, and she frantically shook her head, calling the man's bullshit. Then, I looked to Thanatos, who confirmed with a devious single nod.

"Take him to the back," I growled, slowly standing tall and cracking my knuckles and neck.

The man didn't realize what poor timing he had when he woke up this morning thinking he'd try to take advantage of a prostitute. Didn't know that today, The Boss would return, and he had a lot of anger and bitterness to work out of his system. And soon, he'd feel the full brunt of a Lord of the Underworld's wrath as punishment.

FOUR
THANATOS

HADES HAD ALWAYS BEEN the grumpy sort, and honestly, I'd never been much better. But this purpose, enforcing for a town with a sheriff too drunk half the time to give a rat's ass, to instill fear and take out our jadedness at the world on criminals and low lives? It helped. I knew that spark in my death brother's eyes. He arrived on the surface with an extra itch on his ass, and this first sap had no clue what awaited him on the other side of that door. And me? I'd be right at my King's godsdamned side.

No sooner had we crossed the threshold than the slimy excuse for a human began stammering. "Look, I was drunk off my ass. I didn't mean anything by it."

Hades arched an eyebrow at me and folded his arms. "Ah. Well. Than, please do step aside and let this upstanding gentleman pass. Surely we should throw all accusations out the window due to intoxication."

And now this man made his sentence ten times worse.

Obliging, I slid to one side, knowing the human wouldn't get more than four feet toward the door.

The mortal gave a nervous chuckle and wrung the brimmed hat in his hands, side-stepping toward the door. "You always did seem like the voice of reason, Boss. Much obliged."

Hades's eyes flared with bright blue flames, and the door slammed shut, billowing smoke from its cracks as it sealed with magma. "You're an idiot."

Hades's smoke power wrapped the human's torso, pulling him backward on his heels until his ass met the wooden chair's seat. "Something tells me this wasn't the first time you attempted rape. Isn't that right, Roy?"

Roy's eyes widened, and he writhed in the chair, the animated smoke keeping him locked. "No. No. Of course, not," he stammered, bordering on flat whimpering.

"In fact—" Hades' gaze lifted to mine, motioning with one nudge of his head for me to join them. "Why don't you enlighten us on what Roy here has done, brother?"

Sins and accolades—a deadly continued list we kept on all mortal beings and a burden between Hades and myself—

shared. Hades would sense all they'd done at present, whereas I could see well into their past and even what they *could* do in the future. The Fates ultimately cut the threads for human life, but it was a two-way road with me passing in the other lane.

The curved claws at the arches of my wings crept from behind my shoulders, peering at Roy, threatening him. I walked around him, exposing more of the wings on each pass. "Public exposure and indecency, domestic violence, drunken misconduct on multiple accounts, assault, and not one, not two, not even three—" I flung the wings out, stretching them taut, sending a gust of wind into Roy, toppling him back on the chair. "—but *five* counts of rape."

All color drained from Roy's face, his limbs involuntarily shaking, eyes glued to my wings, unable to decide which one to focus on. "I—I—"

Hades appeared beside him, making the fire blazing on his wings heat to scorching, sizzling against the mortal's skin. He cried out in anguish, writhing against the smoke holding him captive. "How long until he's due, Thanatos?"

Due. For death. The strike of his eternal time clock.

"A year and some months." My face flashed to its skeletal form when it revealed the hour of a mortal's death.

The human's bottom lip sucked in and out from his teeth, tears, and snot streaking his cheeks. "There. See? It's not my time yet. You can't kill me."

Bold mortal. Though I supposed one had to be to carry out the atrocious acts he'd mustered.

"It isn't our job to kill you, mortal." Hades snatched his face within his grasp, tightening his hold, and making the ferocious black claws crawl out, the tips pinching his skin. "We are judge and jury, but only execute what awaits you in the afterlife."

In the centuries I'd known Hades, we formed an unbreakable bond—a brotherhood through death and darkness and knew each other more than anyone else. It was the very reason I peeled back my sleeve, the blackened skeleton's hand replacing my human one, the tiny cracks glowing with radiant orange—ready.

"I don't—I don't understand," Roy stuttered, his eyes darting from the embers floating around Hades's wings to the bones of my skeletal fingers tapping together in a staccato rhythm.

"The river Styx. It's a perfect place for wandering souls to dwell until their fated demise. In that case, there'd be no killing you, only *condemning*."

The mortal gulped and pushed his heels into the ground, trying to put distance him from Underworld King. "I'm not wandering. I want to be *here*. On Earth."

Interesting how misbehaving mortals didn't question our existence. They didn't stare at us in fear from the realization that not only did Greek gods exist, but there indeed was a hell, no matter in what way they believed it to be. They were more concerned about *themselves* and suspended disbelief quicker than a Hermes sprint.

Hades dipped his face into the human's, his pale white face—his true form—appearing, the long white hair floating in wisps around him, falling in length to his hips. "Tough. Shit." Hades twisted his wrist in one direction, obliterating the bones in one of Roy's legs, followed by an arm. Roy screamed, tears streaking his face, his breaths quickening, bordering on hyperventilating.

Hades cracked his wrist in the other direction, repeating the same action to his remaining leg, and finally—he broke one shoulder. "You are to spend what you have left of your pitiful life swimming the river with nothing but your left hand to keep your head above water. And believe me when I say—" A flaming circular crown blazed around Hades's head, his claws digging into the human's cheek, drawing blood. "—this will be *nothing* compared to the eternal punishment I have in store for you when you approach my throne for judgment."

The mortal was too stunned to speak, let alone formulate a coherent response. He wouldn't realize the gravity of the situation until his face began to dip into the soul-infested oily waters of Styx and began to drown. He could never accidentally kill himself, but the constant feeling, the terror at water filling his lungs and mouth, would keep him repeatedly trying.

Hades stepped back, holding a snow-white hand out to Roy. "Brother, would you be so kind as to mark him so the Fates know where to find him when the time comes."

My mortal eyes were such a fiercely dark brown they blended with the blackness of my pupils, appearing entirely black. But darkness filled them whole like liquid onyx when I called on my death god powers. Wrapping a hand over the mortal's shoulder, I held firm, waiting for the ancient symbols to glow like a newly burnt brand over his forehead only to disappear and remain exclusively visible to the Fates and myself.

With the mark made, I stepped back, allowing Hades space for the final step—sending him to the Underworld. There may have been those that felt pity watching the anguish in the human's eyes, the pain shaking through him—a form of remorse despite the unspeakable acts he'd done throughout his life. But I'd long since grown numb to it. See enough hatred and vile behavior humans were capable of, and little guilt remained for those who *deserved* what awaited them in Tartarus.

Clementine's fate. *That* was a harder pill to swallow. Never a more cheerful and kind-hearted human being had crossed my path, and yet murderers, thieves, and liars would outlive her by decades.

Hades lifted a claw to Roy's forehead. "I'll be seeing you real soon, Roy. Bon voyage." And with one flick, leaving a thin line of crimson blood across the mortal's skin, he ported him to the Underworld and into the shallows of Styx to await his end.

"I don't know about you, old friend—" Hades stood tall, cracking his neck to one side as the mortal guise overtook him. "—but I could use a drink."

Fluttering my fingers, I turned my hand back to the human and scoffed. "You think the taste of whiskey on our tongues will cure a damn thing?"

Hades flicked his jacket open, slipping a hand inside. "Nope. Was thinking something a bit stronger." He produced a black leather flask with gold trim.

"Is that what I think it is?" A rare fizzle coiled in my chest.

With a swipe of his palm, Hades unscrewed the top and took a swig, leaving the familiar scents of fermented fruit, honey, and bliss collecting in the air. "Ambrosia wine. Yes."

The only form of light buzz the godly variety could achieve and only one Greek god could create.

"Do you have some unspoken bargaining power with Dionysus I'm unaware of? I didn't think he frequented the Underworld." I held my hand out for the flask.

"He doesn't. But he's still thankful I let him have his mortal mother's spirit for Zeus to turn her into a goddess to live for eternity. He sends supplies with those that *do* frequent the Underworld." Hades handed it to me but snagged it back when I'd taken a drink. "We'll lace the whiskey with it.

Hiding away in a godsdamned closet isn't exactly conducive to intimidation." Hades twirled a finger at the small interrogation room we'd set up in the back of the saloon.

"I don't know. My darkened corner table seems to do the trick." I followed behind him, slipping on my hat as soon as the chatting patron and piano sound hit me.

Hades let out a deep chuckle, securing his own hat atop his head. "You should see yourself in that corner. If it weren't for your white teeth showing on occasion from your grimacing, most would think a demon stalked them from the shadows."

"That—" I turned for my table, twisting on a heel until I could let my ass fall to the seat. "—I can live with."

As dusk melted away through the windows outside, the moon's glowing vibrance replacing it, the saloon filled to the brim until a patron occupied every table. Hades and I took my corner table, mixing wine into our whiskey tumblers and surveying the crowds.

"About to be a golden hour here, brother. Keep a sharp eye," Hades said, edging the hat away from his forehead as he sipped his drink.

"Not to mention a full moon," I grumbled, shifting on my seat and resting my elbows on the table.

A wolfish grin flashed from the shadow of Hades' hat. "Even better."

"I think I get what's going on here now." I leaned toward

my ancient friend, lifting a hand to cover my mouth from prying ears or eyes.

"With what?"

"A certain spring goddess?" I arched a brow at him, waving my hands to signify her curves.

Hades lifted his chin, his eyes narrowing into slits. "What the Tartarus are you talking about?" He asked through gritted teeth.

"You're barely boss at home, so you thrive on it here." I poked the table between us with a forefinger. "Is punishing souls down there not enough for you, friend?"

"You're not wrong." Hades leaned back in his chair with a deep sigh. "But there's an entirely different feeling regarding the living."

A man in a stained linen shirt, red vest, matching scarf, and floppy-brimmed hat stumbled toward our table, already drunk off his ass. Gray stubble littered his chin and above his lip, his bushy white eyebrows like dancing caterpillars. One eye bulged when he pointed at us, smacking his lips together. "You don't look all that scary to me," he directed to Hades.

Brazened or stupid with no room for anything in between.

"Is that so?" Hades rose while I stayed seated and silent.

The saloon had gone quiet, every one giving the nearby table shifty eyes, mouths agape.

The man's lip twitched before he launched his hand to his

holster, and with a speed I was certain felt *far* faster to him, he whipped the pistol skyward, pointing it at Hades. Hades instantly deflected the man's forearm with one of his, while simultaneously grabbing the gun with his opposite hand. With lightning speed, he snapped the cartridge open, emptying it, the bullets clinking and clanking across the table.

Hades slammed the now harmless weapon on the table in front of the dumbfounded mortal. "Now that you're disarmed, why don't you go play cards and mind your own business, or I'm going to tell that guy—" Hades pointed to one of two armed men in opposing corners. "—to shoot you right between the eyes." Hades shaped his fingers into a pistol, pushing his middle finger to the human's forehead. "And no one will do a damn thing about it." He simulated firing the weapon by flexing his thumb and silently mouthing the word "Bang."

The mortal gulped, staring at Hades's hand like it were a real firearm. "Sounds fair to me."

"Atta boy." Hades patted the man's shoulder before shoving him away.

Leaning across the table, I scooped the six bullets into my hand. "I could use extra ammo." Peeling my jacket aside, I shoved each round into the vacant slots in the ammo belt above my holster.

"Glad to be of service." Hades smirked and sat down, shoving both sides of his jacket aside.

Tracing the rim of the tumbler, I glanced at Hades sidelong. "How are you two, though? Really? Seemed to get pretty dicey there for a bit."

Hades growled, guzzling more whiskey and switching to drinking straight from the flask. "I made this bed, and have to sleep in it, Than. There was a time she hated me, a time she learned to love me, and now I feel neither. Which, quite frankly, is worse than hatred—nothingness." He sneered at the word "nothingness."

I'd known the Underworld King long enough; there was little I'd hesitate to say to him and it hadn't changed.

"You know there's a way to separate one's shade from the Underworld, especially if they're a god." I paused, gauging his reaction—a tremor in his cheek and a death stare aimed anywhere but at me. "That is—if you're ready to let her go."

Hades's hands balled into fists atop the table, the snarl bubbling in his throat, making my chest rumble. "Speaking of women. You should follow that." Hades jutted his chin toward the wooden staircase leading to the overnight stay rooms.

Clementine ascended the steps, smiling at me over one bare shoulder.

"Her *room* is up there. Where she *lives*," I spat, snatching the glass into my hand.

"That's precisely the point," Hades replied deadpan. When I didn't say anything, he continued. "You're running out of time to be with her, brother. Go tell her who and what you are, and I think her reaction will surprise you."

"No," I clipped.

Hades' chest puffed. "Don't make me pull rank on you. And believe me, I will. Either you pursue the last chance you have with her or spend the rest of eternity wallowing even more in self-pity over the 'what if.'" He shook his head with one quick swipe. "I won't have it."

"Fine," I growled, pushing to my feet with such force I cracked the table.

With a scowl planted firmly over my gaze, any saloon-goer risking getting in my way would take one look at me and yelp out of the way. My booted feet thudded up each step, and I took deep breaths along the way before pausing in front of Clem's door. My face felt stony before I knocked, and it took everything in me to melt it into something less menacing.

She answered the door a breath later, the surprise in her expression plain. "Than? Is everything okay?"

Nodding, I leaned on the doorframe, crossing my hands at the wrists in front of me. "Everything's fine. Can we talk?" I gestured behind her.

Her throat bobbed with a gulp. "Sure. Come on in." The words came out breathy and wistful, and she stepped aside, allowing me to step over the threshold.

"Thanks," I whispered, my gaze sweeping her quaint

room—a vanity, a fireplace, four post bed with a pink quilt, and a small round table with one chair, a book with torn burgundy cover resting in the center.

"Goodness, I'm so sorry. I'm not used to having people up here. *No* one has been up here except the landlord, in fact." A nervous giggle bubbled through her throat as she whisked around the room, scooping undergarments and stockings, draping them over her arm.

"Clem." I cupped her elbow, stepping behind her, making her draw in a breath and drop everything she held to the floor. "I don't care what it looks like in here. I came to talk to you about something very important."

"Your tone sounds a little ominous." She cleared her throat and turned away from me, slipping a white lace handkerchief from a pocket within her dress. She coughed into it, light specks of blood staining it.

"Here, sweetheart." I handed her a black silk handkerchief with a frown.

She stared at it before slipping it from my fingers. "What's this for?"

"When you cough, the blood will blend into it. No one need be the wiser."

She rubbed the smooth fabric between her palms, eyes cast downward. "How long have you known?"

"A while." I slid my hands under her elbows, coaxing her

not to turn away from me again.

"The doctors say tuberculosis." A smile emerged—faint and melancholy. "And I always thought I'd die of old age with silver hair and wrinkles."

I'd never felt so much pain for a mortal being. There was no way of knowing what the anguish of impending death felt like for a human, and that tore me most. I wanted to take the burden from her or at least share the torture of it.

"Clem, I'm going to tell you something, and I need you to keep an open mind. Can you do that for me?" I circled her skin with my thumbs.

"Of course." Her brow furrowed, her lips pinching together, deepening the dimples in her cheeks.

"I knew you were sick from the first day we met. And knew how long you had to live for a *reason*." I locked her gaze with mine, pinning her in place with it.

Her eyes blinked over and over, her head shaking. "How is that possible?"

"My full name is Thanatos. I'm the Greek god of death." The words echoed in my ears, the wailing cries of the souls I'd sent to Styx pounding through my head.

Her reaction was hard to gauge. I'd expected disbelief, fear, possibly anger, but I dared say she looked contented.

She stepped closer, pressing a small pale hand on my chest. "I should have a harder time believing you, but I—I don't.

Why is that?"

Slipping my hand over hers, I pressed it harder against my chest, yearning to feel her skin against mine but settling for the feel of it through the shirt. "Because your spirit is finding its way home daily, Clementine. Leading you—to me." The black wings appeared, unfurling from their ethereal hiding when in mortal form, curling around us in a hollow embrace.

She smiled at them, gliding over the glossy feathers with her other hand. "Thanatos—" She paused, her smile broadening at saying my name. "—I don't know how much time I have left, and there's something I have to tell *you*."

I folded the wings behind me, moving my hands to her face, palming her cheeks, and staring down at her. "I love you," I stole the words away from her, yearning to say them myself.

Tears filled her eyes. "How did you—then *why* did you— why have you been pushing me away all this time?"

"Because of who I am. Because of knowing you're walking toward your demise. That *I'll* be the one to take you."

Her breath fluttered over my knuckles as a deep sigh pulled from her chest. "Because you think it wouldn't be fair. Wouldn't it be just as unfair for you? Be with me, Than. Just be with me, plea—"

No. There'd be no begging on her part. She should never have to beg for company, for comfort, for love. I'd give her everything I could in the days to come, and when the time arose to send her to the Fields, I'd make it painless, seamless, and put the burden entirely on me.

Cutting her words away, I pressed my lips to hers, groaning at how soft her lips felt against my rough ones.

She gasped and pulled back.

"What is it?" I asked.

"I didn't expect you to feel so—cold."

Running my tongue over my lips, I squared off my jaw. "I should've warned you. It comes with the territory of being—"

"I didn't say I didn't like it. It only took me by surprise." She flashed a sparkly grin, tugging me closer. "Try it again."

I slid my hand to the small of her back, pinning her against me, and kissed her, holding back the power that siphoned life from her, though every neuron in my body called for it. Death was far too close for her—too soon. And there wasn't a damn thing I could do to slow time, to postpone it. Her petite tongue edged the seam of my lips, and I opened myself to her, deepening the kiss and growling into her mouth.

A tingle shot down my spine like someone walking over a grave I didn't possess. I pulled away from her, still cradling her in my arms but focusing my attention on the window.

"Thanatos? What is it?"

Reluctantly letting her go, I stalked to the window, peeling back the curtain enough to peek outside. A man with sepia skin, his long black hair falling to his mid-back, sat on a charcoal-colored horse, a jackal on each side of him. The jackals' eyes glowed green from reflecting the moonlight.

"It's bad news," I replied, glaring at the unwanted visitor to the town.

Anubis.

FIVE
HADES

I'D LET OUT A gruff sigh as Thanatos ascended the stairs in pursuit of the ever-charming Clementine. Telling her who and what he truly was would mean my own identity would soon be outed. Not that it entirely mattered, I supposed. It could be somewhat refreshing for a mortal to realize with whom they shared breath. Not some figment of their imagination or parlor tricks performed by a prestigious magician—the real King of the Underworld himself. But her time dwindled, and Thanatos fooled himself into thinking that wasn't the case. Ignored the putrid stench of death wafting from her like smoke from a burning carcass. She reeked of it. Which meant she had *days* at best.

Time dwindled, and boredom soon overshadowed me. No patron misbehaved, no one stormed in demanding satisfaction from another who'd done them wrong. Quiet as the grave except for the carousing whoops of a group playing cards, others singing off-key to the piano music, and some simply making drunken conversation. I sneered at it all and slipped the hat further over my brow, folding my arms and propping both feet on the table. Perhaps my presence had grown increasingly intimidating over the years, and no one dared to challenge my resolve. Both a curse and a gift. Because I did so love punishing those that deserved it—a recently developed pastime that I used to loathe but lately *looked* for it around every corner.

"Hey Boss," a man slurred nearby, the smell of whiskey and tobacco on his breath.

Not budging, I kept my chin tilted down. "Yes?"

"You uh—you play poker?"

Now there was an intriguing thought.

Smirking to myself, I pulled on the brim of my hat before rising to my full height, tapping a finger against my cypress tree and serpent belt buckle. "You bet your ass I do."

Tobacco Breath snorted and jutted his thumb at the awaiting table with two other men absently shuffling cards and sipping on their drinks. "Deal you in?"

How ironic he unknowingly asked an Underworld god

whom mortals made every attempt to make *deals* with when their time had come to pass into the afterlife. I'd never taken any of them up on it—until now.

"Let's play, gentlemen," I drawled, sliding out one wooden chair with the grace of a passing breeze before flicking my jacket over one hip, revealing half of the six-shooter duo, before taking a seat.

One man with a tweed bowler cap and gray mutton chops let the thin cigar hang loosely from his mouth, shooting sidelong glances at his counterparts. "Think this is a good idea, boys?"

"Why not?" I slid the hat from my skull, resting it on a table corner, and dragged both hands through my chin-length locks. "Are any of you cheaters?"

Mr. Chops shook his head and tossed his cards to the pile in the center. "No, sir. I'm as lowest life as they come, but I ain't no cheater."

A deep chuckle bubbled from my chest. "At least you're honest. I can respect that."

An audible gulp sounded from the mortal to my right, a portly fellow with a full bushy red beard. With shaky hands, he reached past me to relinquish his own cards while the drunk man who'd invited me to the table palmed the sea of cards, re-shuffling them.

"I ask that *he* deal the cards." I pointed at the drunkard, who guffawed but let his smile fade once no one else joined in the laughter.

Mr. Chops furrowed his brow, removing the cigar long enough to stare at me slack-jawed. "Bobby never deals. It's always Frank." Chops pointed at Red Beard when referencing Frank.

"Good for you, Frank. But I said I want Bobby to do it." I growled my last words, making the table rattle and flashing a blink of fire in my gaze, challenging them to decline me one more godsdamned time.

Mr. Chops cleared his throat, rummaged the cards together, and slid them in front of Bobby. "Ain't that hard, Bob. Just deal us each five cards and one or two when we ask for 'em to be switched."

"Yeah. Sure," Bobby mumbled, attempting to glare at me but failing miserably.

Leaning back in my chair, I kept my gaze steely, panning from one human to the other as each player tossed in their ante chips and Bobby dealt the cards afterward. They each picked them up one by one, adjusting them in their hands as they arrived. I waited until all five of mine rested before me and scooped them, only taking my eyes away from them long enough to gauge my luck.

A wicked grin begged at my lips, but I kept my expression neutral—two kings, of spades and diamonds, in hand with only the pursuit of a third.

"Name of the game is jackpots, boys. Jacks or better to open," Frank announced, still taking the partial helm of the dealing job.

Stacking my cards, I lightly tapped them against the table, waiting for anyone to start the betting. When they all kept still, I grabbed a chip and tossed it to the center. Turns went clockwise, with each man betting and throwing down cards to trade. I launched two cards at Bobby, purposely hitting his arm with them, making him skittish. My blood simmered beneath my skin, eyeing the third King needed to call triplets.

More bets continued, some calling, some folding, but Bobby—dearest Bobby—*raised* the stakes. It was the singular fuck up I'd been waiting on and the reason I'd asked him to deal. With a mortal like Bobby, an opportunity to gain some rep by beating the big bad Boss the one week he was in town? He couldn't pass that up.

"I'll raise," Bobby mumbled, tossing several chips into the pot.

Tapping a single finger on my turned-down cards, I raised a brow. "Pretty confident, hm, Bobby? That's quite a raise you did there."

"For all you know," Bobby started, shuffling his cards in his hands with a tongue poking at the corner of his mouth. "—I could be bluffing."

He wasn't. And it didn't take see-through vision to

mysteriously view all their cards—which I couldn't do without trying—but intuition? Knowing how to read people? I'd done *that* for centuries.

"Too rich for my blood," Frank spat, throwing the cards on the table with a whistle.

Mr. Chops shook his head and followed suit.

I locked gazes with Bobby, giving him one final chance not to do what he was about to do—*cheat* against the King of the Underworld.

"Call," I demanded.

Bobby blinked and let out a nervous bout of laughter as he looked at the other two men. "It wasn't your turn, Boss."

Leaning forward, I kept my fiery gaze focused on him. "I said, *call.*"

Mr. Chops gulped and nodded, nudging his nose at the table. "Better do what he says, Bob."

Bobby's knee bounced below the table, his eyes shifting between the two mortals but unable to meet my gaze. "Fine." He laid the cards on the table, neatly overlapping each other. "Read and weep. A royal flush." He smiled widely at the men's shocked faces, but before his fingers peeled away from the King of Spades, the corners flamed, scorching his skin.

Bobby yelped and jumped in his seat, staring at me wide-eyed, assuming *I* was the one that made his card spontaneously combust.

"How in the hell," Frank said, trailing off.

Making a *tsking* sound like one would do toward a house pet, I placed a finger on the king card. "Seems the powers that be aren't happy with this card, Bobby."

"What the hell are you talking about?" Bobby held his burnt hand to his chest. "It's a king card, same as any other."

"And any other turn of events would have you hopping out of here a richer man, but not today, Bobby." I displayed my cards, a matching King of Spades glaring back at him. "And I know none of you will call *me* the cheater."

Chops leaped with such force it sent his chair flying backward. "Bobby, what the flying fuck?"

Flipping the hat over my arm, into my hand, and onto my head, I rose, smoothing the lapels of my jacket. "Keep the chips, boys. And Bobby, something tells me what they plan to do to you for cheating is far worse than I could, but—" Moving past him, I slid a hand over his shoulder, sending an uncomfortable heat surging through his jacket. "I'll see you in a few years." After patting his arm, I flashed a fanged grin and moved for the bar.

The bright moon disappeared behind a cloud outside, and dozens of scattered whispers that didn't emanate from the bar patrons polluted my ears. No sooner had I squinted toward the swinging doors, Thanatos appeared behind me, Clementine in his wake. She eyed me curiously as if seeing me for the first time, a certain admiration in her gaze.

Good. He finally told her.

Thanatos leaned toward my ear, lips dropping to it. "It's Anubis."

"What?" I spat. "What the Tartarus is *he* doing here?"

With a thumb, Thanatos flicked the leather piece securing his pistol in its holster. "Don't know, Boss. Care to find out?"

After a curt nod, I flipped my jacket over both holsters and shoved a palm into the swinging doors. Thanatos asked Clementine to stay inside before following.

"Well, I'll be damned," Anubis' deep voice echoed from the shadows, the lilt and twists in his ancient accent still as present as they were centuries ago.

After lighting a cigarette, I rested one hand on a pistol hilt and glared at him through smoke tendrils. "Aren't we all?"

His gray eternal pet jackals sat on either side of the pewter horse he perched upon; his forearms crossed over the harness. A vibrating chuckle shook from his belly, and he urged the horse closer, a nearby hanging street lamp illuminating a face I hadn't seen in over a hundred years. He had a perfectly angular slanted nose, deeply tanned complexion, thick black eyebrows, bone-straight hair falling to his mid-back, and a glacial pair of blue eyes that cut at you like a jagged icicle.

"When I heard talks of these so-called 'Lords of the Underworld,' I didn't think it'd be *you* two," Anubis spat, chewing on a piece of straw and letting it hang from his teeth.

Thanatos kept silent, standing still behind me with his shoulders drawn back.

Smirking, I calmly pointed at each jackal. "Nice dogs. Mine's bigger."

The jackals each made a light yip before letting out subdued growls and baring their teeth at me. I flashed my own canines, fire igniting in my gaze.

"At least mine wouldn't take out half the town center with a single step should you have brought him to the surface," Anubis retorted, making clicking sounds at the jackals to make them quiet and sit.

I took a long drag of the cigarette. "That's because Cerberus has a job beyond simply living art deco around me wherever I go."

Anubis' steely cobalt stare narrowed.

"What the Tartarus are you doing here, Nuby?" Thanatos asked, the impatience in his tone plain as he said it through gritted teeth.

Anubis winced at Than's nickname and shook his head. "I control half the surrounding towns, and I've come to claim territory that's rightfully mine."

"And just what do you think gives you that right? Considering the 'stature' we hold, I'd say typical rules and regulations don't apply here," I countered.

Anubis's jackal form appeared over his face for a breath of an instant, too quick for a mortal eye to catch, but he knew *we* would. "I wasn't asking, Underworld scum."

His attempts at intimidation were amusing at best.

"What would you want with this town anyhow? You have your people. We have ours," Thanatos chimed in, his hand squeaking on his pistol's hilt creeping into my ear.

"Something tells me we want mortals for different reasons."

An uneasiness tightened in my gut. "What different reasons could there possibly be for death itself?"

"There's more to life than death, Underworld King." A crude seriousness muted Anubis's expression, his horse scraping its hoof against the dirt.

Thanatos's hand turned skeletal, his heels gripping the ground with sheer frustration. "Care to not speak in riddles?"

"The End of Times will need a vast army. And I'm determined the Egyptians will survive it." Anubis sat up straight.

"The End of Times? You mean that little 'ol thing that's been threatened for centuries and has never actually happened?" I scoffed, tossing my spent cigarette near my boot and extinguishing it.

"Eventually, it will. How confident are you in how long the Greeks will hold up? If at all." Anubis's voice lowered, eyes darkening with fierce sapphire.

Thanatos slid forward, his jacket tearing at his shoulder

blades as the arches of his wings edged out. "We don't need an army of dead mortals with primordials and three king brothers in our ranks."

Slipping a hand over my death brother's shoulder, I coaxed him back before we had far more to explain than a few random bursts of fire or eerie fog. "How many godsdamned soldiers could you possibly need? You must be up to the millions now."

"It's the *end* of times. You should want an infinite amount at your disposal as well."

"*How* do you have that many?" Thanatos asked, his wings settling back into his godly skin. "Not every mortal *I* even send to the afterlife goes to the Greek Elysian Fields or Tartarus. You couldn't possibly have that many traveling to Duat."

Anubis smirked, his gaze falling to his horse and absently petted its neck. "You know as well as I do when mortals are sent to the afterlife, they go to the realm they most remember or bear a connection. And more and more are forgetting altogether of the Egyptian variety. My army numbers are dwindling and suffering for it. You Greeks, as well as countless others, have *plenty* to share. How many souls swim through Styx, hm? What purpose do they have now?"

I chewed my bottom lip, a tick tremoring through my cheek. "Why demand to take over the town? You said it yourself. You control all surrounding territories."

Anubis moved his hand toward his hip, causing us to move

our palms to our pistols. "I've taken all that are capable from them. I need new blood."

"You're taking them before their time is *up*," Thanatos growled.

Anubis edged his hand closer to his side. "*All* mortals die. What's a little sooner rather than later?"

"You're not touching this town. They all deserve to play out their lives no matter their destinies," I spat, surging every kingly power within me to sense each of Anubis's movements.

"I see. I'm going to have to try a different method with you two." Anubis slung his pistol from its holster, aiming it at an older man who'd hobbled out of the saloon.

"Jacob," Clementine screamed, storming from the saloon and toward the older man as if she intended to block him with her body.

Thanatos snarled, curled his arm around her shoulders, and shielded her behind him. In the same moment, we lifted our pistols, aiming them at Anubis.

Anubis's attention diverted from the man focused now solely on Clementine. "Aren't you the prettiest little dying mortal?"

As Clem had called him, Jacob appeared obliviously drunk to the situation, squinting at us and swaying on his heels.

Thanatos moved Clementine further behind him, the snarl bubbling in his throat, jacket tearing from the wings again. "Fucking leave, *now*."

"We should not be damn well doing this in the middle of *town*," I added, spying on saloon patrons ogling us from the windows.

Anubis nodded, decocking the hammer of his pistol and pointing the barrel skyward. "You're right. For once. And to show you what an upstanding gentleman I can be, I'll allow you all to settle this the Western way."

"Out with it," Thanatos snapped.

"A duel," Anubis started, pointing a finger at *me*. "With him. Two days from now. Pistols at dusk."

"Fine," I clipped.

I made no plans to lose.

"Very well," Anubis said with a jackal's smile. "I look forward to humiliating you in front of your people, god-king."

"Yeah? I'm sure it's been a while since you've seen Osiris. I look forward to reuniting you with him." We hadn't lowered our pistols, and I gripped the handle tighter, glaring down the barrel at him.

Anubis cackled into the night wind, turning his horse and flanking jackals in the other direction, disappearing into a dense wall of smoke and fog.

Jacob flailed his hands toward the fog and hobbled away, babbling incoherently.

Thanatos holstered his weapon and took each of Clementine's shoulders within his grasp, a tinge of panic and fear I'd never seen on my brother's face. "Clem? Are you alright?"

"Whew," Clementine batted stray strands of chocolate hair from her eyes. "I don't know about you, but I could use a dance."

Thanatos's brow creased, and he leaned back. "After what you witnessed? After Anubis almost killed someone in front of you?"

Clementine shrugged, reaching for Thanatos's hair, letting it run through her fingers like oil in water. "Even more reason for it. But the biggest one? I want to dance because I'm *alive* Than."

A frown pulled at my lips, an unease making me rub a forming kink from my neck.

Thanatos sighed and pulled her to him, embracing her and stroking her hair.

"How about it, Boss?" Clem asked once they'd parted from the hug.

Astonishing how she didn't so much as wince or eye me oddly now that she knew I was King of the Underworld. "I'm a taken man, darlin'. But Thanatos, I'm certain, is more than up to the task."

Clementine's eyes glistened, gazing at Thanatos with a brightness that hadn't seemed possible given the darkness settling around us. "Than?"

Than nodded and slipped his hand with hers. "Sure, Clem. Anything you want."

"I'm going to hold you to that," Clem replied, smiling at

him as they headed into the saloon.

I leaned on a post, watching them through the dingy windows from outside. They danced to every song the pianist played, whether it be a jig or slower, but the grin never faded from Clementine's lips. She threw her head back in laughter several times, enticing more smiles from the god of death than I recalled from his existence. I could only hope he made the most of the *days* she had left.

In the meantime, I cast my gaze to the moon peeking from parting clouds, contemplating how to put a leash on a jackal known as the Egyptian death god. That was until my thoughts were interrupted by the bank across the street exploding in a furious blast of fire and smoke.

SIX
THANATOS

It became increasingly difacult to deny Clementine anything she asked. Even if I'd felt it in her best interest, her days grew shorter, and the cosmic pull because of it only swelled more and more within me. And so, despite the number of times I'd danced throughout my godly existence were few, I agreed to her request and felt my skin heat at the brightness pulsing in her gaze.

"I've gotta warn you, sweetheart. I'm not exactly the lightest on my feet," I grumbled, my fingertips tingling as she slid her hand into mine and pulled me into the saloon.

Hades tipped his hat at me, electing to stay outside and watch after Anubis's impromptu visit. I didn't blame him in the least and wouldn't have disagreed.

"You can't be that bad. What about the two-step? I'll even let a few steps on my toes slide. But past three and these puppies will have to surrender. Shoes can only take so much, hm?" Her eyes took on an ethereal sparkle from the dim candlelit lamp lighting surrounding us. Her smile broadened as she took both of my hands, creating a rectangle between us.

Snickering, I let some of my black hair fall over my gaze, relishing in the subtle lip bite it always enticed from Clem. "Where on Earth did you come from, Clementine?"

Freddy played far too lively of a jig for my taste at the piano, and for every two steps Clem took, I took one, but let her balance on me and spin circles as she saw fit. "I'd say the same place as you, my mama, but, I don't even know if you have one?" She raised a thin dark brow.

The question gave me pause, hand stiffening against hers.

"I'm sorry. I shouldn't have asked—" She halted dancing, droves of drunken men and saloon girls still rotating around us like a chaotic carousel.

"No, Clem. It's not that. I've—" Lifting her hand above her head, I twirled her once, twice, and the third time, I pulled her chest against mine just as Freddy slowed the tempo. "—I've never had anyone ask me."

She flattened her palm against mine, a shaky breath pushing past her lips. "I did."

"Yes. And only a mother." I slid my free hand to her lower back, pressing it there, imagining how her porcelain skin would feel against my palm—smooth, soft, and warm.

Her throat bobbed, and she inched closer, letting me lead her in a round of twirls and circles, waltzing the dancefloor between the open spaces of others. "Only?"

"It's a lot to explain. But she's a goddess of the night. And created me to serve my divine purpose—" I caught her gaze, sliding my hand between her shoulder blades to hold her to me, praying she didn't pull away with my next word. "—death."

Her large eyes blinked before focusing on my chin. She made no attempt to turn away, nor did her grip lessen on me, and finally, she nodded, a petite smile gracing her lips. "Wow. And here, my mama was just a lowly seamstress."

A breath pushed from my lungs. "And no less important. If she were anything like you, I'd say far more necessary than darkness overtaking the earth."

Clem's eyes went glassy, a single tear streaking her cheek. "She was. Daddy always used to say I'm the spitting image of her."

All the gods above and below let their connections align so they could meet in the afterlife.

Dampening the frown etching my lips and forehead, I used a thumb to swipe the tear away. "We're celebrating life today, Clementine."

Before she could question my meaning, I entirely wrapped my arm around her, lifted her feet from the ground, and continued the waltz with her suspended. If we weren't in public, I'd have loved nothing more than to float us *both*, showing her my wings that I had no doubt would mesmerize her.

Perhaps...there would still be time.

Infectious laughter burst from her chest, her cheeks turning a shade of cherry blossom as the world spun around us. A smile forced its way over my lips, and there proved little effort to stop it. Her outlook on life and gleaming demeanor, despite riding the coattails of mortality, filled the craters formed in my soul, ignited a hope I never knew existed, and reassured me that whatever destiny had in store for me—there'd be as equal of light to counteract the shadows.

"Than, I'm so dizzy," she cried out, slapping a hand over her closed eyes, still giggling against my shoulder.

Slowly coming to a halt, I let her slide down my body until the tips of her shoes met the wooden floor. With two fingers, I peeled her hand away, lowering my face to hers, desiring to kiss her with every spark in my body. But I couldn't find it in me—couldn't burden her with it.

"Hey," Clem whispered, placing a hand on my cheek. "You alright?"

A short burst of a laugh tore from my chest that I couldn't hold back. A dying woman, a sick woman, who knows I'm the god of death, still found it in her heart to question my state of mind.

Cupping her chin, I grinned at her. "Peachy, Clem. But you, don't mind me saying, look a bit tired. Want to call it a night?"

"Honestly?" Clem pursed her lips and grabbed my arms, curling them around her in an embrace. "No. I don't. Can we stay like this a little longer, Than? Even if it's a ragtime song, I just wanna *sway*."

I'd ensure wherever she wound up would have a flower field vast enough for her to run, dance, damn well somersault through if her heart wished for it.

Nodding to her, I coaxed her head to my shoulder and swayed with her wrapped in my arms and one hand smoothing her chocolate hair.

"I imagine you've been to all kinds of places. Heard all kinds of music, hm?" Her light voice was slightly muffled by my shirt.

"I have. Any country, in particular, you're curious about?" One finger found its way to the exposed flesh at her nape, tracing over her collarbone and the hollow at her throat.

A sensual moan purred from her throat, and her temple nuzzled my shoulder. "Spain. I've *so* wanted to know the sound of flamenco music. Is it as vibrant as the way they dress?"

"Definitely," I whispered into her hair, moving my hand

to her shoulder for her to feel my fingers. "The guitars here in the west, while resonating beautiful sound, the strings are far stiffer than they use over there. The guitars in flamenco music flutter and glide like the dancers do." Flicking my fingertips against her skin like she was the strings, I flashed a fanged grin at the sight of gooseflesh forming.

"That must sound gorgeous," Clem cooed, her arms tightening around me.

"And sometimes they use what are called castanets." I continued trekking down her arm, lightly tapping my middle finger and thumb as I traced downward. "They make a fast-paced rhythmic clicking sound that pairs with the beat they keep with their heels."

Her tiny fingertips lightly tapped against my shoulder in time with the beat I kept. "You describe it so beautifully I can almost imagine it."

Maybe she wouldn't have to imagine it. Perhaps I could play it for her. I had the power—had the means.

An explosion blasting outside made us stand straight, killing any sense of mood developing. Clementine shrieked, her hand flying to her opened mouth. The piano music came to a grinding halt, and all bar patrons froze, all conversation fading away. When nothing followed the explosion and no harm came to the saloon itself, everyone returned to what they were doing as if nothing happened.

Frowning, I turned to Clementine and squeezed her hand. "I'll need to help investigate that."

"Duty calls," she repeated from before, a weak smile edging her lips. "All this excitement has me a bit run down anyhow. Think I'll go take a lay down."

Stepping closer, I pressed a kiss to her forehead. "Go rest, Clem." After stroking my knuckles over her cheek, I made my way to the exit.

"Hey Than," Clementine beckoned. Once I caught her gaze, she continued, "I'll be in my room for the rest of the night—" Her eyelids became hooded. "—if you feel so inclined to continue our conversation."

A tingle sparked in the base of my spine, an invisible fist hitting me straight in the gut. I'd been around long enough to recognize the lust playing not only in her eyes but packaged around her words like a delicately wrapped gift topped with a sparkling bow.

Playing a vibrant heat in my stare, I gave her a single nod with all intention of visiting her once Hades and I were through. She gave me a brightened wide smile and a small wave before ascending the stairs.

I couldn't be sure of all she wanted from me, and even less sure how I'd push past the guilt if she desired *everything*. But I owed her my company and time, and she'd have it.

Smoke tendrils leaked from the bank's windows when I

crossed the street outside. Hades had already made his way into the building, and the Sheriff entered the same time I did, clad in only his hat, red long johns, boots, and a rifle in hand.

"Sheriff, you don't need to be here for this. Go back to bed," Hades ordered, pointing at the door while squinting at the damage to the vault wall.

The Sheriff bristled, resting gun barrel on his shoulder, his other hand flying to his hip. "Now listen here. This is still my town, and if there's an explosion, the Sheriff should be there to inves—"

Hades shot him a glare, fireballs pulsing in his eyes. "I *wasn't* asking."

"You know—" The Sheriff cleared his throat, adjusted himself, and shuffled backward. "—I think I'll go get some more shut-eye. You boys got this handled just fine."

Hades crouched by the vault door blown from its hinges, the ball safe still intact and supported on its metal box with pegs. "This doesn't make one lick of sense."

"Agreed. Why would anyone in their right mind try to rob a bank in this day and age when a stagecoach is far easier?" I knelt by Hades, rubbing some of the residue between my fingers. "And this isn't from dynamite."

"Their dynamite wouldn't be strong enough to damage this door anyway."

Rising, I moved into the vault, circling the untouched safe.

"And why stop at the door? What was the point?"

"No matter what kind of explosives they used, they wouldn't have had any luck doing damage to this safe." Hades stood beside me, gesturing to the safe's circular shape. "Hard to affix anything to it, and it'd diffuse any explosion."

Snickering, I kicked my boot against one of the metal legs beneath the box. "And if they tried separating the ball to deal with it later, they'd have to figure how to not only drag several hundred pounds out of the building but also cart it off somewhere without getting caught."

"Exactly. And there's no way a mortal would've been fast enough to high-tail it out of here before I arrived." Hades shifted his hat back to scratch his forehead.

"You thinking this was Anubis?" I stared at the black stain on my fingertips. "Could be ash."

A growl bubbled in Hades's throat. "I *know* it was Anubis. His subtle, yet not subtle, way of letting us know he can mess with us. Fuck with our town."

"Want to retaliate?" Wiping my hand on my pant sleeve, I surveyed the damage to the vault door, estimating the town's cost for repair. We could quickly fix it with a snap of the fingers, but there hadn't been a soul who didn't at least hear the explosion. It would've been a far more complicated to explain than random bursts of fire from Hades's palm.

"No. I should pay Anubis a visit. Try to talk some

godsdamned sense into him before someone in this town gets hurt or *worse*."

"Tonight or first thing in the morning?"

Hades leaned on the doorway, pointing his finger at me like a six-shooter. "*I* will go in the morning. But I need *you* to stay here if he tries anything stupid."

"I don't know. Two is better than one if you're trying to intimidate him into backing down." I hooked my thumbs in my belt loops.

Hades smirked. "Trying to say I'm not intimidating enough on my own, brother?"

Truth? Hades had never been what you'd call "ruthless" by any means, but in the past decade he'd lost some of his edge. I'd never dare say it to his face.

"I wouldn't dream of it."

Hades gave a slow nod and pushed from the wall, making for the exit. "Besides, Thanatos, *you* have a bed to warm tonight. And women don't particularly like you sneaking out of it in the morning when you fancy them."

"Eavesdropping on me now?"

We stood, touching elbows at the edge of the deserted nighttime street.

"Tartarus, no. I recognized that glint in her eye. She has it for you bad, brother. Seph used to look at me that way." Hades's jaw set, he sniffed once, and his gaze cast to his boots.

"Have you thought more about what I said, brother?" I kicked a stray pebble.

"No," Hades snarled. "And I won't until I'm back. Ruins my mental holiday. Understand?"

"Loud and clear. Loud. And. Clear." Scratching my chin with the tip of one thumb, I gave the Underworld King a curt nod.

Hades adjusted his hat and jutted his head at the saloon. "Good. I'll talk to you tomorrow."

I'd made all motions to move, walk, or even take a single step toward the saloon, but my heels suddenly cemented to the ground. What waited for me in that building was nothing short of bittersweet bliss. And she'd *invited* me. Considering I hadn't given her any inclination that I declined, I'd be a horse's ass to bail now.

Drifting through the bar area felt like a passing memory. I knew I'd walked through it, navigated around tables, and avoided tripping on outstretched legs, but I could scarcely recall how and when I arrived at her door. How long had I been standing there? How long did I stare at the wood grain frozen like a frightened deer at the other end of a rifle?

Clenching my teeth, I knocked three times on the door. Thirty seconds went by, and when there was no answer, I assumed she deeply slept and turned away. But the door creaked open, and her beautiful face, drowsiness still hanging in her gaze, appeared from the crack.

"Howdy, stranger," she whispered, smiling at the sight of me.

Mustering every nerve I had, I leaned on the doorframe, grinning. "Howdy. Still want company?"

Her smile broadened, and she pushed the door the rest of the way, stepping aside to allow me entry. I removed my hat before crossing the threshold, tossing it between my palms. The door clicked shut behind me, the sound of the lock tumbling into place, making my usually cool skin catch on fire. She appeared in front of me, a serene expression gracing her face, all signs of tiredness melting away as she gently took my hat, placing it on a nearby rickety wooden table.

Candlelight bounced jagged shadows across the whitewashed walls and lavender bedspread. But when she stood at a precise angle, the sepia light cradled her like a halo, bordering her hair. Her slender fingers found my knuckles, tracing over them before resting her hands on my forearms.

"I can't give you forever, Clem." The words forced their way from my throat—rigid, strained, and gritty.

She moved closer, coaxing my arms around her, her palms landing on each side of my face. "Neither can I, Thanatos." A smile brushed her lips. "But I don't *need* forever. I *want* right now." She rose to the balls of her feet and brought her mouth to mine.

I engulfed her with my arms, encircling her lower back and shoulders, and kissed her. The tiniest whimpers fluttered from her throat, followed by the tip of her tongue tracing the seam between my lips. I moved one hand to bunch in her hair, bending her backward as I deepened the kiss, our tongues twining.

Olympus forgive me for what I was about to do because gods above—I *wanted* this too.

SEVEN
HADES

TO AVOID APPEARING OUT of thin air in the middle of another city, I purchased a midnight black horse and trekked to one of Anubis's controlled outlying towns. It had been eons since I dealt with another death god. We usually kept to ourselves, upholding our duties as the Universe deemed, and stayed out of any other god's way. Anubis clearly had other plans that threatened to dissolve our unspoken truth. I never considered Anubis to be meddlesome or villainous like Eris or Moros. But then again, I'd never call him "righteous" either. He rode the fine line, stepping on whichever side suited him best at the present moment.

Slowing my horse to a lazy trot, I lit a cigar when the first pair of townsfolk eyes landed on me. The black hat shadowed most of my features—as I preferred—and I used just enough power to conjure the floating embers and ash. I'd often wondered what it felt like for a mortal to be in the presence of a god. We gave off a certain aura unique to our divine nature that I knew didn't compare to any other human reaction or emotion. Once in my vicinity, they'd sense something different, something similar to Anubis. And, because nothing sensible could be rationalized, they'd brush over it but keep me in their sights.

Resting my hands overlapped on the saddle's pommel, I flashed a fanged grin at a group of women scurrying past and whispering. "Mornin', ladies," I drawled, tipping my hat to them.

After several fluttery bouts of laughter, they looked away from me and continued down the street. My hips shifted left to right with each stride of the horse, my spurs lightly clanking from the vibrations, boots resting on the stirrups.

"Any stranger showing up in town gussied up in all that black ain't but one damn thing—bad news," a man with stringy peppering hair, wide-brimmed nose, and a chunk of chewing tobacco puffing out one cheek said before spitting at the ground.

He'd been far enough away a set of mortal ears wouldn't have heard him. His expression melted from smug to sheer terror when I stopped the horse in front of him, leaning forward with narrowed, fiery eyes. "And here, I haven't even had the chance to make your acquaintance yet."

The man stared at me and accidentally swallowed tobacco, coughing and hacking once it hit the back of his throat. Another man stood beside him in a well-kept blue vest with a silver pocket watch. His brown handlebar mustache swayed as he clapped the other man on the back several times. Satisfaction settled in my bones, knowing all I needed to do was show some teeth and fire in my eyes to intimidate a mortal. It was about as comforting as nuzzling into Cerberus's fur.

"You keep swallowing your baccy like that, Benny, and you're bound to right poison yourself," the man with the handlebar said.

Shifting my eyes to the only human of the two able to speak, I willed his attention. "I'm here to see your boss. Mind pointing me in that direction?"

Handlebars crossed his arms and squared his chin at me. "Depends. You here lookin' for trouble?"

A chuckle rumbled from my gut. "Quite the opposite. But I assure you, if I had any ill will toward your town, we wouldn't have this conversation." I flickered an image of my true self to him, a blink of glowing eyes, long white hair, fiery crown, and burnt wings.

Handlebars pointed at a large building with cracking red

paint, his finger shaking along with his knees, soon rattling his entire body.

"Much obliged," I said—smooth and deep.

Tsking at my horse, I lightly clipped his side, turning him toward the said building with a light tug on the reins.

Behind me, Benny's coughing subsided. "You look like you done seen a damn ghost."

"Nah. More like a demon or some shit."

Wincing, I let my eyes fall closed with a disgruntled sigh. I'd been called several names through the ages, and few bothered me, but demon? It couldn't have been further from the truth, primarily when you oversaw them within your ranks. It'd become downright insulting to be associated at their level. You might as well call me a damn harpy.

No sooner had my boots hit the dirt, I tied the horse's reins to one of the nearby hitching posts, the familiar scent of ash and death hitting me like a backdraft. All death gods exuded the same pungent aroma. The Universe's way of allowing us to identify each other while in disguise, I figured.

Flicking my jacket over the twin pistols on each hip, I slammed a palm into the swinging doors. It didn't take long to find him considering the Egyptian god sat on a black and gold throne in the middle of the abandoned saloon like a godsdamned patriarch. One jackal sat to his left side, Anubis scratching its head, while the other lay at his feet, curled into a ball and sleeping. Anubis leaned back in his seat, a leg draped over one ornate armrest, not moving a muscle or bothering to flinch upon my entrance.

His teeth gleamed white in the dingy lighting of the room, cerulean eyes not lifting to meet mine but rather fixed on the jackal. "Wondered if you'd show up before the duel. Petty attempts to change my mind and all that, hm?"

"An intuitive god. Such a unique trait." I matched his grin, leaning my weight to one side and hanging a hand from a pistol handle. "Surprised your little pooches aren't nipping at my heels."

Anubis's glacial gaze met mine, his smile turning feral. "Because I've told them not to—for now." He tapped his head with two fingers.

"Aw. Don't gotta stand on ceremony for little 'ol me." Shifting closer, watching one jackal's eye pop open to follow me, I ran a finger across one table, rubbing the thick dust coating between two fingers. "You'd think a man would care a little about the upkeep of his makeshift fortress. Or at least let them still run it as a saloon." I grimaced as a cobweb stuck to my hat's brim and batted it away.

"They have three others." He held up the same number in fingers, wiggling them and making the surrounding torches glint in his many rings. "And my time in each town is short. No need to outstay my welcome."

"Something tells me you're not welcome in most towns, Anubis. No matter how long or short you stay." Smirking, I leaned a hip on the table, hands at the ready near my pistols.

"You find the concept of death amusing, Underworld King?" Anubis gripped the bulbous edges of one armrest, both jackals assuming mirrored positions on each side of his throne.

I bounced a corner of my lip. "No. But you don't take it seriously, either. Otherwise, you'd let *fate* do its damn job and wait on your precious godsdamned soldiers when they're good and ready."

Anubis tapped one ring against the metal armrest before slowly rising to stand, black swirls forming at his feet. "I never took you for the type to follow all the rules, Hades. What pleasure can there be for a god condemned to rule death, to surround themselves with it, if not to *bend* the rules now and again?" Each jackal snarled, standing with their master, backs hunching and the fur on their spines standing on end.

"The sacrifice we make for our power—our eternal lives." The edges of my ember wings peeked from the jacket, and I shrugged it off, letting it fall in to the wooden floor.

Anubis shook his head, eyes glowing a fierce electric gold. "To sacrifice means you *chose* to do it. Divinity *forced* it on us, we didn't choose shit. And we either abide by nature's desires or become nothing but stories and stardust." He made a fist, hand pulsing orange. A shimmering gold sekhem scepter appeared in his hand, and he slammed the butt end to the floor.

"You want to do this? Think no one would take a peek through the windows?" Clenching my teeth, I kept the wings folded back despite every instinct to flare them.

"I do want to do this, Underworld god." Anubis opened his hand, sending wafts of black smoke mixed with tendrils of red toward the windows, obstructing the view. "I really do."

Heat zipped down my spine. Snarling, I flexed my arms, the ember wings bursting into flames behind me. "Fine."

Anubis held the scepter in one hand, raising his opposing arm to form a small rounded shield—blackened with an etched golden jackal laying with its head held high, varying hieroglyphics surrounding it in a circle bordering the shield. "Stay," he commanded the jackals.

They stopped growling and retreated backward, mimicking the pose of the jackal on Anubis's shield. Anubis pounded the floor again with the scepter, producing a matching helmet in the shape of the ancient canine depiction.

Conjuring fog and smoke from the river Styx, I willed it to circle my arms. "Afraid I'll scar that dashing face of yours, Duat god?"

"Not on your eternal life. I like the feel of it pressing against my skull." Anubis twirled the scepter until it was poised atop his shield and aimed at me.

My pointed black claws crawled over the top of my

fingernails, and I flapped the wings, hovering above Anubis and thankful for the saloon's high ceiling. Anubis cocked his helmeted head to one side, resting the scepter across the top of his shoulders, legs moving in a strategic circle. Launching my hands forward, I sent spikes of my gray power, aiming for Anubis's side. Anubis lifted the shield, blocking, and countered by twisting on his heel, swinging the scepter underhanded, the point of it carving through the air near my hips. I narrowly dodged it and glared down at him.

Anubis surged forward, and I clapped my hands together, sending a rippling torrent of smoke catapulting toward him. He flew backward, colliding with the dusty bar and leaving a godly-sized hole in its front. Each jackal still perched on the floor by his throne made their eyes glow yellow, lips curling, but they remained where they were.

Anubis let out a feral growl as he pulled himself from the wreckage, swinging the scepter back to his shoulders. "That's the first and last hit you'll get on me, Styx."

I'd always been a proponent of the saying, "Actions speak louder than words," so I said nothing. Anubis used the curved hook on his scepter to snag on my shirt, yanking me to ground level. Using both hands, the shield secured with leather straps to his arm, he swung left to right, sideways, vertically, and every which way. Utilizing my wings to hover, I plumed surges of smoke to block his blows, occasionally letting it fuse around my limbs to use my arms as makeshift shields.

Anubis swung the scepter over his head, landing a blow on one wing, enticing a grunt from me. The wing's arch blazed orange, burnt feathers rustling like they had conscience thought. Anubis charged forward, slamming the scepter's head into my chest with repeated quick thrusts until my back slammed into a table, breaking it in half. Clenching my fists at my sides, digging the sharp claws into my palms, I rolled my shoulders and swirled the fog in my grasp, building up its energy.

As soon as I burst it toward Anubis, he slammed the butt of the scepter to the ground in front of him, a thick wall of ash forming and blocking my power before fluttering through the air and disappearing. Having no weapons in any form of ethereal arsenal like Hephaistos kept, I improvised by producing a sword made from the very fire pulsing through my wings, the pommel lashing streaks of flame over my knuckles.

"Fog power not doing enough for you?" Anubis asked, launching another barrage of frenzied thrusts, overhand and underhand swings.

I dodged, blocked, and counter-attacked his movements, slicing my flaming blade through the space between us when I saw the opportunity and jabbing it forward once given a chance. What started as a "civilized" battle of power soon catapulted into a contest on who could throw each other the farthest and cause the most damage. We could continually beat the shit out of each other with no way of ending the other's life, with no proper way of harming one another permanently, but the stabs, punches, and colliding with hard surfaces still hurt like Tartarus, and we *knew* it.

Anubis whipped off his helmet, tossed aside the shield, and punched the scepter against the floor with both hands, snarling a word in ancient Egyptian. His jackals sprung to life, eyes glowing orange, crackles of lava forming in their skin, taking the form of hieroglyphics. They hurdled toward me, sprinting and snapping their jaws.

Fanning my wings and swirling my arms toward the skies, I produced a mimic of Cerberus using the foggy smoke to form it. The three heads bared their teeth, eyes a furious crimson. "No," I roared at the canines with Cerberus towering behind me, taking up nearly the entire space. The jackals halted, skidding back on their hind legs before scampering to Anubis.

Anubis leaned on his scepter, his gaze wandering over the three-headed smoke dog behind me and landing on his jackals hiding behind his legs. "How in the fuck did you manage that?"

"I told you. My dog's bigger. Takes a more assertive authority." Waving my hands, I willed the smoke back to Styx.

Anubis turned a full circle, examining the destruction we caused. "I suppose it's somewhat of a good thing. I'll already need to explain why it looks like a hurricane ripped through here. Wouldn't be much left were we to continue."

Conjuring a cigar, I lit it with a snap of my fingers, producing the flame, and took a long drag. "I assume there's no persuading you? Going to make us still do this absurd duel?"

"You call it absurd." Anubis crouched and scratched each jackal's head. "I call it respect. We're about due."

I'd never come to blows with another death god. Had never been challenged by one but the establishing a pecking order borderline intrigued me.

"Alright. I'll participate in your little duel, but I'm setting some terms." I sat on the edge of a cracked table with folded arms.

Anubis stood, his jackals content to sleep at his feet. "Fair enough. Name them."

"We do it fair and square. We limit any usage of powers. If it's enough to warrant mortal attention, it's out." I scratched my chin with my knuckles.

Anubis gave a curt nod. "Agreed. Anything else?"

"When I win this—" I pushed from the table, walking closer to him. "—you set your damn eyes elsewhere. Our town is *off* limits. Understood?"

Anubis's eyes brightened and he raked a hand through his dark hair. "And when I win—the town is mine. Understand *that*?"

It wouldn't come to that. I'd use every fiber of my being, every neuron, every possible minute power I had in me to ensure that did *not* happen. Our people trusted us and I'd be damned if I let another death god spoil that.

"Understood." I held out my hand. "Do we have an accord?"

Anubis stared at my palm for a beat longer than necessary before slapping his skin against mine, ash fusing with ember between us. "We have an accord."

"I'll see you soon, *Duat.*" After throwing the cigar to the floor, I extinguished it with my boot as an extra 'fuck you.'

Anubis chuckled, watching my boot shimmy left to right. "I look forward to putting you in your place, Hades. About time someone did because it sure as shit won't be Thanatos."

I fitted the black hat back on my head. "Thanatos and I have a close-knit past, unlike you and Osiris. Something I wouldn't expect you to understand given stories say he *replaced* you."

The corners of Anubis' jaw tensed and he flicked his hand toward the exit. "Please *do* let the door hit you on the ass on your way out."

Tipping my hat at him with a fanged grin, I strolled out of the saloon. I'd be the first to admit we were matched for power, but having leverage always helped. And his leverage was Osiris. I'd use every ounce of it to my advantage and do what I always did best—my fucking duty.

EIGHT
CLEMENTINE

THANATOS WOULD BELIEVE THAT this connection I felt for him boiled down to my pull toward death with each passing day. He'd wither it to such generic reasoning, but I couldn't describe what I experienced whenever I was around him with any explanation other than—love.

I couldn't be sure what, if anything, he'd felt toward me, but given his actions, and his words, there was a fondness there, and I needed to make him realize that loving me back wouldn't burden me. If anyone were getting the raw end of the deal, it would be him because—my time was limited. No one had ever shown me such acts of selflessness.

And the fact he showed up tonight told me he wanted

the same thing—the opportunity, *any* chance we had to be together despite him being a god, despite my bitter mortality. A Greek god. It astonished me how easy it'd become to forget who he was, *what* he was. Because standing in front of me, *I* saw was another tortured soul who wanted nothing more than to give affection and receive it.

I slowly pulled away from the kiss, my eyelashes fluttering against his cheeks. Thanatos's chilled knuckles grazed my face, and he pressed a kiss to my forehead. "Are you staying, Than?" The question came out far more desperate than I'd intended.

"Not going anywhere, sweetheart." His hand slid to my lower back, and he began to sway, his boots scraping the scuffed wooden floor. "I'm all yours tonight, through the morning, and every waking moment you have left."

My sinuses stung, tears threatening, but I gulped them away. The melodic sounds of a stringed instrument, unlike anything I'd heard before, floated through the room. Thanatos slid behind me, coaxing my arm to raise and placing my hand on his head. He continued to sway with his hips pressed against my mid-back.

"Is this—" The idea of music playing without instruments, music I'd never heard before and had no way of knowing its sound, made words escape me.

"Flamenco music."

A tear escaped despite my best efforts at holding them back, my spine stiffening as I fought more from rolling down my cheeks.

Thanatos moved his other hand to my stomach, outstretching his palm and putting a kind of pressured comfort there. "Don't hold back on my account, Clementine. You want to cry? Sob. You want to yell? Scream to Olympus. You deserve to *be* however you feel."

I listened to him, letting the tears streak my face and doing nothing more to stop them. His lips grazed the nape of my neck, soft, repeated kisses over my skin as he continued to sway us, fingers tapping against my abdomen once the rhythmic clicking sounds began in the song. With slow, tender care, he turned me around to face him, keeping one arm around my waist and taking the opposite hand in his. He danced us around the room, and I became a different person—carefree, sensual, and undying.

Panning my gaze over each of his shoulders, I recalled the rumors that'd spread about him, and now knowing his true self, one stood out in particular. "Than, do you—" The question gave me pause. Would it be rude to ask?

"Do I what, sweetheart?" He pinched my chin between thumb and forefinger, caressing me. "Ask me anything."

Melting into his touch, used to its comforting chill now, I sighed. "Do you really have wings?"

His midnight eyes glistened in the dim lighting, a shadow of a smile tugging at his lips. "Yes."

"Really?" I breathed out, eyes widening, trying to imagine what they'd look like at their full span. Would they fit in the tiny confinements of my room? "Can I—"

Thanatos's fingers slid up to my lips, silencing me. After pausing, ensuring I stayed quiet, he took a step back, undoing his belt and slipping his hands under the hem of his shirt, freeing it from his body. My throat and center tightened at the sight of him—bronzed skin, carved large muscles, each molded to perfection. The arches of two glossy black wings peeked over each of his shoulders, wickedly curved talons at the tips. Keeping our gazes locked, he flexed both forearms, making the wings fan out, the onyx feathers bristling and stretching.

Gasping and clasping my hands over my mouth, I stepped closer, eyes affixed and mesmerized by the majestic sight. "They're beautiful," I whispered, fingers wiggling against one another, ravenous to touch the feathers.

As if reading my thoughts, perhaps he could, Thanatos gently took one hand, grazing his shoulder with my fingertips, and placed it on one wing behind him. "Go ahead, Clem."

Tears blurred my vision, and with a shaky hand, I traced my fingers over each sleek feather, softer parts bunched in between overlapping patches. Thanatos's eyes closed, muscles tightening the closer I got to the arches, the wings vibrating against my touch. I bit my lip, switching between focusing on the wings and his reaction to what I did. Swooping my hand over one arch, I moved closer to the curved talon, but Than snatched my wrist, his eyes lazily opening.

"Careful. I don't want them to cut you." He kissed the inside of my wrist, pulling me closer until my breasts brushed his bare stomach.

It suddenly became hard to breathe, anticipating what was about to happen—and who it'd be with—*death*. But no matter how hard I forced myself to mull it over, the idea of it gave me no further pause than if any other man stood in front of me. Only excitement, lust, and an overwhelming impatience to feel his weight on top of me remained.

"Are they that sharp?" With fresh confidence, I trekked my fingers up his stomach, committing every groove between muscles against my skin to memory.

His hand trailed over my shoulder, dipping to the dress's fastenings at my back, flicking them away one by one. "Lethal."

His fingers now grazed the bodice beneath the outside fabric. The wait itself to rid me of a dress I wore nearly every waking day, and albeit gorgeous, would torture me to no end. "Would you think it uncouth of me to ask you to—" I locked his eyes with mine, my cleavage pumping up and down. "—rip it?"

A devious grin lifted at one side of his mouth, a glint of sharpened canine sending a twisting bout of lush knots surging through my stomach. He clutched both parts of the bodice, and with one quick tug, it left my body, and he let the remnants fall to the floor behind me. I stood with my breasts on full display, the dress's skirts still clinging to my bottom half. My nipples instantly hardened from the coolness in the room, and I nearly salivated over Thanatos's gaze taking all of me in, his calloused fingers tracing across my ribs and moving to my breasts, cupping and kneading them within his large grasp.

A moan escaped my throat, and he dipped his mouth to my neck, kissing, licking, and nipping the skin before devouring my mouth with his, pressing my warm body against his cool one. His arms wrapped around me, followed by the wings enveloping us, creating an obsidian canopy with flickers of candlelight peeking through the cracks.

"You are, beyond a shadow of a doubt, the most beautiful woman I've ever seen." He circled my cheeks with his thumbs, wisps of his dark hair tickling my skin.

The words tugged at my heart, given the centuries, the thousands of years he'd been alive. And even if it were untrue, he felt keen to say it to me, and so I wouldn't dampen it by replying with the first thought that'd come to mind—and you have so much more to see in your eternal life. He'd find someone to make him happy after I left this world. I was sure of it. But whereas I didn't fear death, it pained me to think Thanatos would let future love slip through his fingers because of me. Now wasn't the time for that conversation. However, even if it were on my deathbed, it had to be said to him. He deserved serendipity as much as any mortal being, including myself.

Smiling and nuzzling my cheek into his palm, I for now replied, "You're not too bad yourself, cowboy."

Thanatos folded the wings behind him, resting them there to my pure delight because I wanted to stare at them all night if he'd let me. "Come here, my sweet Clementine." He walked backward, extending his hand for me to take and leading us toward my bed.

He knelt in front of me, slipping his hands under the skirts. His fingers trailed up the sides of my shins, leading to my thighs, and taking the dress with him. His palms scraped my ribs, and the curve of my breasts until the skirts were lifted over my head and tossed in a heap with the bodice. We both remained silent, settling into the moment and savoring it. He stood tall before me, moving his hands to his belt, but I reached for it, playfully flicking his grip away with a shy smile.

He burned me with his gaze as he let his hands fall away, allowing me to take over. His raven hair fell in enticing tendrils, framing his face and casting an ominous yet sensual shadow over his features. Not daring to move my eyes from his, I slipped my fingers into his pants and tugged them down, pausing as they slid over his butt—perfectly muscular and rounded. I stifled a gasp escaping my throat at the sight of him, his *length*.

Thanatos slid a hand over my collarbone, cupping the back of my head and pulling me to my feet. His lips crashed with mine, and our mouths became a frantic bout of swirling tongues, pressing lips, and antsy grabs that couldn't settle on a singular place to touch each other. Turning us in a half circle, I felt the bed press against my calves and soon after, I was in his grasp and at his mercy as he lowered me to the mattress. Looming over me, he kept his grip on the back of my neck, the wings rustling once as they shifted further behind him.

My entire body shook, an agonizing mix of sultry anticipation, shivers from his chilly skin pressing to mine, and an overwhelming bout of nerves.

"Clem," Thanatos whispered into my hair, settling between my legs. He trailed his fingers down the center of my forehead, over the bridge of my nose, and caught a fingertip on my bottom lip before encouraging me to nibble and suck on it.

"Yes?" I hardly recognized my own voice, a huskiness lacing the word that'd come from another side of me, one I never dared show in public.

"Will you have me?" Thanatos used one hand to push against my right thigh, spreading me wider, the tip of him teasing my clit with velvety swipes.

The shivers subsided once I saw the fire blazing in Thanatos's gaze. I scraped my nails up his bulging arm muscles, reaching one hand to caress a wing. "I'm yours, Thanatos." Lifting my hips, further presenting myself to him, I pressed a warm palm to his icy cheek. "*Take* me."

A growl bubbled in the back of his throat, primal and strained. The tip of his length pressed to my entrance, and I tensed, focusing on relaxing instead as he pushed the rest of the way inside me, already making me cry out. My eyelashes fluttered, my body steadily acclimating to him, his sheer girth. He held still and tweaked a nipple between two fingers, swirling his tongue around it once it became an aroused pebble. My back arched from the bed, nails digging into his shoulders, leaving indented marks on his flesh.

He rocked forward once, twice, and the third time he filled me to the hilt, our hips slapping together in unified harmony. A smile begged on my lips, a warmth pooling in my chest and traveling to my core. He hitched one of my knees, allowing him to plow into me deeper, claiming me with each frenzied thrust. Thanatos slammed a hand to the headboard above me, keeping my body in one place as he drove, pumped, and bucked his hips.

"Oh, my—" The familiar buildup of tingles and swirls tickled my insides, gooseflesh forming over my arms and legs, toes curling.

Thanatos didn't stop, his wings slowly curling around us as the sensation built and built before I came undone, screaming in pleasure I'd never experienced as a human being. Sweat soaked my forehead, more than usual, but I paid it no mind, my insides clenching around him. Thanatos grunted, his hand clutching the headboard. He continued thrusting in and out of me, but the speed slowed—almost insufferably. The wings fanned to each side of us, and his body left mine, his length disappearing immediately.

The darkness in his eyes spread beyond his iris, overtaking part of the white, and he remained silent, pulling me to sit and turning me so my back was to his front. One of his tanned arms wrapped around my stomach from behind, pulling me flush against him, guiding my slit over him, and filling me again. I arched my back, rolling against him with every rock he pushed forward. He kept one hand around my hips, pulling me on and off him, while the other reached from underneath to massage my breasts, his enlarged canines nibbling my shoulder.

A softness fluttered the tops of my thighs, his wings curling and delicately flapping along with the rhythm we kept. The feathers caressed my arms, fusing around them like an embrace. The hand that tantalized my nipples slid down my stomach until it reached my center. Thanatos used two fingers to tease my clit, pinching, rubbing, and caressing.

"Come undone for me again, sweetheart," he whispered against my neck before swiping his tongue over my skin. "Because I'm not finishing until you're boneless in my arms." Thanatos pressed the bridge of his nose against the side of my head, fingers rubbing with more fury between my legs. "You take every ounce of pleasure you wish from me. And then take some more."

And he meant every word of it. We made love through the wee hours of the night beyond the point of stamina I thought I possessed, especially given my condition. He pleasured me with his length, tongue, and fingers the while the wings caressed me, adding extra euphoria into the mind-numbing mix. When I'd fallen slack against the sheets, he stilled inside me and groaned through his release, a pained look in his gaze and all-out shuddering as if he hadn't been with a woman in decades.

We lay on our sides with him behind me, his arm draped over my breasts, lips grazing my ear. The tickle and burn itched my throat, and I coughed, a small amount of blood staining my fingers.

Thanatos kissed my shoulder and produced the black silk handkerchief he'd given me, sighing into my hair once I took it and wiped the blood away, dabbing the corners of my mouth afterward. "I took it too far. I should've never—"

Shutting him up, I reached a hand behind his head and brought his lips to mine, knowing he wouldn't care if they tasted a bit like copper. "Stop, Than. I'm fine. I'm honestly surprised I didn't cough a lot sooner."

He rested his chin at my nape, his hand resting on my hip, and his fingers drumming like flamenco music. "I told you I'd make it as painless as possible."

"Are you saying—" With eyes unblinking, I turned to my back, staring up at him in awe and disbelief despite the ebony wings perched behind him. "—did you get rid of my symptoms somehow?"

"Lessened them. It can get excruciatingly painful, Clementine, and you don't deserve it. I can't save you from death, but can at least make it peaceful." He swam a thumb over my cheekbone, an anguished smile appearing.

"Thank you," I croaked, a tear blurring my vision that I didn't try to hide. "Is it possible for you to—show me how it'll be? A taste?" Distracting myself from the sheer embarrassment of asking him, I traced the feathers of one wing. "I don't want to be scared, and I figured—"

"It's alright to be scared." Thanatos interlaced his fingers with mine. "Death is inevitable for all living things, and mysterious and unknown. But there's beauty in the endless cycle of things—death is necessary for an ongoing universe."

An invisible horse sat on my chest, weighing me down and tightening my heart. "That's beautiful. If I knew even a sliver of what to expect, I could be more prepared for it. How many mortals get the chance?"

The chance to *know* a god of death. To earn his friendship and love. And to gain his affection in return?

Thanatos's brow cinched, his gaze falling to our chests

pressed together before he nodded. "Alright. But it would help if you tried and not be frightened by what you see. I will glamour it as much as I can, but my powers won't allow me to disguise it fully."

Scared by what I saw? A new swirl of nerves whipped a tornado in my stomach, and I hiked up a knee, pressing it against his arm. "Why would I be frightened?"

"I'll look like me but—different. You can close your eyes if you wish." His eyes searched my face, an unspoken hope that I'd not do just that—look at him the entire time and make that connection with him despite the life being taken from me.

"No. I'll be fine. I *want* to see you, Thanatos."

Nodding again, he adjusted the pillow under my neck and slid a hand behind my head. The other gripped my chin, steadying me. He moved over me, settling between my hips like we'd done countless times earlier, and gazed down, whisking hair that'd fallen in my eyes away. His lips parted, coercing mine into doing the same, and a bone-chilling iciness surged through my chest, darting to my face. His eyes turned completely black, two liquid pools of onyx, lifeless yet glistening with energy. The skeletal parts of his face revealed in patches—his cheeks, near his chin, partially on his forehead. I stared up at him, feeling something of me siphoning from my body into his, tendrils of blue curling from my mouth only to be consumed by the god of death. Though painless, it numbed me, my head growing dizzy, and a hollow throb formed at my temple. A small blue butterfly flapped to Thanatos's shoulder, its wings pulsing in time with his. My fingers dug into his arms, though I could no longer feel their coolness, and in the same instance, he let go and sunk back on his haunches.

"I'm sorry. I shouldn't have gone so far. The pull is—" Thanatos frustratedly dragged his hands through his hair, tugging on it as he remained kneeling at the foot of the bed and not looking at me.

An added weakness weighed heavy on my bones, but a fresh light outshone it. "Because it's getting closer." Shifting, I knelt before him, peeling his hands from his head. "It's alright. I appreciate how calming it's going to be, Thanatos. I wouldn't even know it was death if that's how it felt the whole time."

"That's my intention." He pressed his lips to my knuckles before pulling me to him in an embrace. "What do you wish for now?"

There were a million things I could wish for but only a handful were obtainable, even for a Greek god.

"To fall asleep wrapped in your arms and wings?"

A gentle, genuine smile spread over Thanatos's lips, and he lay us on our sides, doing as I asked with both arms and wings, blotting out most of the candlelight. I nuzzled against him, concentrating on the sounds of our steady breathing as it lulled me to sleep. When a mortal died, they didn't simply become sustenance for Earth, didn't merely disappear, only to be forgotten once all living families met their end.

Death *wasn't* the end. That in itself was comfort enough.

NINE
HADES

ANUBIS. I SHOULD'VE KNOWN the asshole couldn't be reasoned with. What had I expected traipsing into his town making ultimatums? No matter. I didn't fear not being able to best him in a power-dampened duel any more than I believed he did our job better than I. The townspeople were my number one concern, and I only wished to save one of them, *any* of them, from getting caught in the crosshairs—literally in this sense.

I'd been delighted to enter the saloon the following morning to find Thanatos's usual corner vacant. I could still sense his presence, which told me all I needed to know—he was upstairs with the dying fair maiden. As hard as I knew it'd be for him when it came time to usher Clementine to the afterlife, I knew it'd be far more difficult for him to deal with the eons of questioning were he to have never taken the time given to them. But I would be there to help pick up the pieces, the same as I always had since Nyx brought him to me as a young boy, and presented him to me without question as part of a peace offering between the Olympians and Primordials. Only the gods know what would've become of him if I hadn't adopted him then and there. I raised him as my son, and as the centuries passed, we became more like brothers than anything else.

It didn't happen often, but today remained relatively quiet given the town's usual crime activity or domestic indifferences. Since I only got a week per season to act as the "Boss Enforcer," it sometimes made me antsy and bored. Thanatos remained upstairs, and I didn't dare disturb him. I could handle anything that came through the door, be it an outlaw or Erebus himself. Though his assistance always made the jobs easier, and, let's face it—a lot more fun.

Playing my third game of Solitaire, I scooped the cards into my palms, shuffling them as I scanned the room. The bartender wiped down the bar top, organized bottles, and mugs, and leaned on a railing when he ran out of chores. Because of the early hour, only two customers sat at a table in the center, spouting off farming and cowboy stories but mostly complaining more than anything else. With a deep sigh, I slapped the cards to the table, sipping on a tumbler of whiskey simply to taste it on my tongue.

A portly man burst through the swinging doors, his floppy hat shoved to the back of his head, his white cotton undershirt stained brown at the top from leaked chewing tobacco. Dirt coated his face, his hands, and a pistol dangled haphazardly from a half-worn holster and belt at his hip. He pointed at me, green eyes wide, a hunk of tobacco shoved into his cheek. "You," he spat.

I continued to play my game, knowing whatever this man was about to say was worth about as much time as trying to lick a horse's hoof. "Me," I responded coolly, not bothering to look at him.

"You killed my cousin," the man yelled, arousing curiosity from the two patrons but not the bartender.

Still not raising my gaze, I organized the cards and sipped more whiskey. "You'll have to be more specific."

The man boldly moved closer. "Phil Harkham. He owed the Crump Brothers a gambling debt, and one of 'em brought him to *you* lot."

Resting the cards on the table, I leaned back, interlacing my fingers. "I recall him, yes. You have an issue with the way we conduct business?"

"Damn straight I do," the man roared, shaking his fists. "Murdering a man for some measly gamblin' debt?"

The two patrons gave side-long glances before rising and

shuffling to the opposite side of the saloon.

Funny enough, Thanatos was the one who sent the man to me several days before his expiration date. But I welcomed his sorry ass when his knees landed on the banks of Styx for what he did.

"*Only* a gambling debt, you say?" I smirked and lit a cigar, puffing on it several times to further piss the piece of shit off. "Have any idea what *else* your precious cousin did?"

The man scrunched his nose at me like I was Cerberus licking his balls. "Why the hell would I care?"

"You should." I glared at him through the curling smoke, flashing fire in my gaze. "Maybe if you'd cared a little more, he wouldn't have stabbed a woman to death in an alley to steal a few horseshoes."

The man's expression flipped from mortified to denial instantly, and he reached for the pistol at his hip. "You're a goddamn liar."

The world slowed around me as I used my divine-given powers to launch from my seat, grab the pistol as it came out from the holster, and disarm him, bashing him in the face with the hilt. To the human eye, it would've happened far too quickly to make much sense of it. The bartender ducked, and the two patrons dove under the table.

"Fucking Christ," the man bellowed, holding his bleeding and broken nose with both hands.

"I'll give you precisely three seconds to rethink your decision to attack *me*. You choose poorly? I treat you the same as your cousin and feel no pity over it." The words came out as a pitted growl, fueled by years of suppressed aggression, tension, and a flippant disregard for a quarter of humankind. After emptying the revolver's ammo, I threw the pistol across the room, far enough that if he tried to retrieve it stupidly, I could stop him.

The man held his hands out, taking tentative steps toward the exit. He shifted his eyes to the bartender peeking over the bar top, feverishly shaking his head at him.

Was this fool actually going to *run* away from me?

With a bob of one brow, I froze his boots in place.

"What the—" the man stammered, his arms flailing like a windmill when he couldn't move, almost bending backward to the floor.

Sliding forward until we stood toe-to-toe, I circled at the ground. "Strange. Must be molasses or something."

"Where would molasses come from in a damn bar?" The man grabbed one leg and then the other, pulling at them to no avail, face turning red from the strain.

"Your time is up. And since you've failed to answer me and chose instead to run away like a coward, I think a visit to my office is about due." I jutted a thumb beyond me at the ominous door within the shadows.

"Look, no, I—" The man winced and covered his face with

his arms as if slapping him should be the least of his worries.

"Well, well, I see you've been keeping busy," Thanatos's voice droned behind me.

Stealing a glance at him, I smiled at the sight of Clementine perched under his arm, cheeks rosy and a grin as wide as Texas. "Only reminding folks why they should fear us, Than." I patted the still-cowering man's head.

After Thanatos kissed Clementine's cheek, he sidled up and dropped his lips to my ear. "He's got a good twenty years on him, brother."

Groaning, I shoved the man, making him fall onto his back, boots still stuck to the floor. "*Of course* he does."

"Don't mean it's got to be an *easy* life," Thanatos suggested, bobbing his brow.

"Careful now. You're starting to sound as sinister as me." Snickering, I crouched by the man struggling to sit upright. "Deaf or blind, cowboy. Three seconds. Choose, or I choose for you."

The man's eyes bulged, and he sat up on his elbows, bone slamming into the wood as he tried to sit up. "What? No. No, please. I'll leave you alone. You'll never see me again. Promise."

Shaking my head and *tsking*, I made smoke billow from my mouth like an angry dragon. "You really should make better use of your time." I placed a hand over his face. "Blind it is." Removing my touch, I stood tall, adjusted my hat, and released his feet from the floor. The man's eyes clouded over, and he shrieked.

Clementine's face went pale, staring at the tragic man writhing on the floor. Frowning, I stood by Thanatos and re-buttoned my jacket sleeves. "Escort him off the premises, would you?"

"With pleasure," Thanatos nodded, tipping his hat. "By the way, I take it the Anubis thing didn't work out? Bet he was a prick about it too?"

"You know him all too well." A light gasp escaped Clementine's throat as I drew near and stood my ground. "I'm sorry you had to see that. I often forget about bystanders when I'm—doing my duty." My glower deepened. "He's a bad man, Clementine. Just as bad as his cousin was. In the damn family genes, it seems."

"But—" Her eyelashes fluttered, and she moved closer, smoothing her hands down her dress. "—is what he did bad enough to warrant making him blind?"

I ran a hand over my beard several times, contemplating how to word this not only to a mortal, but one with a vibrant soul. "It's not about what he did. It's about what he'll *do*. At least that'll make it harder for him. Maybe even less devious."

Clementine stepped close enough that her bare arm brushed my jacket sleeve, and her voice lowered. "But if you know they're going to do something evil, why let them live?"

An age-old question that the gods themselves questioned regularly, but one we could only summarize in one definitive answer.

"It's not my place, for one. And for two, unlike other death gods, I see that their fated lives are to fruition. If we take them too early, who's to say they would've done that deed if they're destined for an afterlife in hell because they did evil in their living life?" Removing my hat, I raked a hand through my hair. "And that means, darlin', a bad soul could wind up in the wrong place, souring it for the others. What kind of eternal bliss and justice does that serve?"

Clementine blinked, her lips rubbing as her gaze shifted to Thanatos returning inside. "I never thought of it that way."

"Don't beat yourself up over it. Mortals don't intend to know what awaits them after death, so they live their truest lives. But you?" I bumped my shoulder against hers. "You're an exception."

She beamed at me, and Thanatos appeared at her side, rubbing her arms.

"Why don't you two go for a stroll? Get lost or something." I flicked my wrist at the windows displaying a picturesque view of the buildings across the street, the sun rays bursting through the buildings, sky as blue as cornflowers.

Thanatos raised a dark brow, his eyes shifting between

Clementine and me. "Dusk is soon. I assumed you—"

"Oh, I want you here. But dusk isn't for several hours. Go on. I got this covered." I nudged my chin at the exit and slid a chair from the table.

"O—kay," Thanatos said tentatively, placing a hand on the small of Clementine's back, ushering her forward. "I'll meet you outside, sweetheart."

Clementine flashed Than a pair of sweet, sultry eyes before moving through the swinging doors and to the dirt road outside.

"What exactly am I supposed to do on this *stroll* you've suddenly committed me to?" Thanatos pressed a hand to his chest. "Do I look like a man who regularly goes on *strolls*?"

Clapping my brother on the shoulder, I guided him toward the doors. "Bring some alcohol, stop at the grocer for picnic food? Tartarus, maybe ride some damn horses? You'll figure it out. But most importantly, enjoy that sun for me, hm?"

Thanatos's eyes formed slits. "That's a low blow."

"Not when it's the truth, Than." I gave politely shoved him at the doors and waved at Clementine through the front windows before moseying to my awaiting seat.

Time passed with no interruption, minus the usual saloon chaos that only threatened patron livers and lungs. As thankful as I was for the town's respect, I also, as screwed up as it was, craved confrontation. An Underworld King could only play so many games of Solitaire before he felt compelled to condemn someone or pass judgment. Boredom plagued me, and I made a chunk of wood appear in my palm beneath the guise of the table, a whittling knife in the other.

I'd sat for several silent heartbeats, contemplating what I wished to carve. I settled on a narcissus to give it to Persephone upon my return as a peace offering—another one. As far apart as we'd grown, we were each other's forever, and there was nothing I could do to change that, or relatively nothing I'd be *willing* to do. And so, I'd continue to work back into her favor the same way I had for centuries since I brought her to the Underworld. It was on me. It always has been and always would be.

After an hour of carving, paying close attention to minute details such as cracks in the petals and the curve of the leaves, I held a completed wooden narcissus flower. Once back in the Underworld, I'd add magic to it, making the flower glow incandescent yellow, before handing it to her. Securing it in my pocket for now, I squinted outside at the setting sun. The sky took on shadows of violet, fiery orange, and pale yellow as dusk settled in, casting an amber glow border around the darkened clouds still scattering the horizon. A breath later, Thanatos entered the saloon with Clementine on his arm.

"Perfect timing," I teased, lighting a cigar and pushing off the table to stand.

Thanatos squeezed Clementine's bicep before letting her go.

She gave his cheek a quick peck and hurried to the bar to grab an apron and serving tray. "Figured I'd get you all worried I wouldn't show up."

An unexpected chuckle roared from my belly. "You're anything but a man who goes back on his word, Than. Nice try."

"Not sure how I feel about being a loyal lap dog," Than retorted, frowning.

Shaking my head, I rested the cigar between my teeth and shook both of Than's shoulders. "Cerberus is the dog. *You* are a loyal friend, and it's something I've always admired about you. Plus—something we have in common."

A gray fog floated outside, darkening the saloon and impeding the sight of the buildings across the street—Anubis and his godsdamned entrances. Even *I* didn't stoop that low.

Thanatos glared at the window before sprinting to Clementine, asking her to stay inside while we gods sorted out our differences. I peeled back my jacket, grazing my fingers over each hilt of my twin pistols, the grooves of each etching. With any luck, this would be dealt with in time for supper, and Anubis would crawl back to his territory. And with even *more* fortune, we'd never have to see him again.

Anubis emerged from the smoke, those glacial eyes glowing blue beacons luring prey to its demise. With each step he took closer to the saloon, the fog and smoke settled until only enough to skirt the ground remained. He chewed straw, glaring at me as I strolled through the swinging doors, slipping on my black hat and ensuring the twin pistols were on full display. Thanatos followed me but stayed beside me while I met Anubis in the street, facing him.

"Thought we agreed this was between you and me, Hades. What's your lackey doing here?" Anubis asked, staying still but motioning his head at Thanatos.

Thanatos silently folded his arms, glaring daggers into Anubis's skull.

"Calm down, Duat. He's only here to make sure you stay on the straight and narrow. Can't have any—casualties." I widened my stance, making a flame flicker over my knuckles.

Anubis chuckled, eyes darting to the flames before returning to my face. But his gaze averted to Thanatos before he spoke. "We have something in common, you know, death god. I, too, carry the dead to their afterlife, but Osiris gets all the credit." Lazily, methodically, Anubis's eyes returned to me.

The nerve comparing me to Osiris had my ethereal blood boiling beneath my skin.

"Whatever you're trying to do, it isn't going to work," Thanatos replied, his tone gruff and aloof.

Anubis flashed a smile, flipping the straw to the other side of his mouth. "Such a good boy."

Thanatos slid a foot forward and I shot a hand out to halt him. "Stand down, old friend. Don't let this shit for brains rile you up."

Snarling, Thanatos retreated, flaring a finger at Anubis and pointing at him. "You make this a fair fight, or I will pound your ass to the Earth's core."

"Well, then. I might do it on basic principle because *that* I'd love to see."

"Stalling now, are we? Let's get this over with. I've got better things to do than tongue lash with you on a vacant dirt road," I snapped, flicking my hands at my sides, readying them near the guns.

"The joy it will bring me to usher *your* people into my army. Yes, let's get straight to it." Anubis grabbed the straw and tossed it to the ground. "Shall we say ten paces? And make sure you play fair. Some of us don't have the luxury of two pistols."

Grinding my teeth, I gave him a curt nod. The smug expression had yet to leave Anubis's face, and it only threw more oil into the raging inferno swarming within me. Saloon patrons lined the windows inside, hiding behind panels but peeking enough to see the show. We turned on our heels, backs to each other, and made vast strides in opposite directions.

Seven steps. Eight. Nine.

On the tenth, I perked my godly ears to alert me when Anubis reached for his weapon, a trick I'm sure Anubis would do himself. Hearing the flick, I whipped my pistol from its holster, turned, and fired from the hip. We both landed shots—

in the other's jacket, leaving bullet-sized holes—a draw.

Anubis shot a glance toward the windows filled with townspeople, and when his gaze floated back to me, he smirked and fired another round.

"You son-of-a-bitch," I yelled, removing my other pistol and firing several rounds at him as I side-shuffled to cover behind a wagon. "Should've known you'd play dirty," I shouted, peeking around a wheel.

Thanatos remained by the saloon, hand reaching for his weapon, and I held a finger up, shaking my head for him to stand down. I needed him *there* to protect those inside. And who knew how long this firefight would last? We could take bullets without harm, other than it hurting like Tartarus, but we would have to explain why we didn't bleed.

"Don't take it personally, Underworld," Anubis yelled back, ducking behind a water trough. "Only business."

Leaning to one side, I raised both pistols and fired, narrowly missing Anubis's shoulder as he leaped behind the trough. Growling, I sat back, holding both barrels skyward and taking several deep, long breaths.

"How's that Queen of yours, by the way?" Anubis yelled. "The blonde? Heard you and she aren't getting along so well lately. Brother to brother, mind if I have a go when she's through with you? Always did fancy gold."

I gripped the hilts of guns so harshly my arms shook,

knowing full well Anubis's game at every waking fucking turn. Manipulation. Mind games.

"How is Anput these days? Or wait—is it Bastet today? Tomorrow? I could never keep track," I roared to him, tilting my chin upward to shout it to the skies.

The sound of the hammer clicking echoed in my ears, and we stood in unison, firing bullet after bullet, side-stepping in time with one another and dodging every shot before all barrels were spent. We halted, staring each other down amidst the tendrils of gun smoke wafting from our pistols. Anubis smirked and launched his hand to his back, removing a small hidden Derringer pistol, aiming at me. I'd thrown my guns to the dirt, splaying a hand, ready to surge fire into him even if it meant the whole damn town seeing. I could *not* let them see him defeat *me*.

A sudden shot rang through the air, the tiny pistol in Anubis's grasp launching from his hand and burning his skin. Thanatos? But no, Than stood in his same spot, staring wide-eyed at—the Sheriff. He held a smoking rifle, standing tall in his red Long Johns. He spat tobacco on the ground, still aiming the gun at Anubis with furrowed brows.

"If you're tryin' to get some kinda respect from us doin' this whole song and dance, you best look elsewhere, boy. Because the Boss here? And that fellah behind me? They are the only ones runnin' this town."

Anubis rubbed his hand, hiding the scorch marks already healing themselves and disappearing. He shot me a glance first, followed by one at Thanatos and finally landing on the Sheriff. "Mighty brave of you to fire that thing at me. And even braver, you're still aiming it."

"Don't bother me none." The Sheriff cocked the rifle. "These two won't let you hurt me."

Nearing the Sheriff, I coaxed the rifle down and patted his shoulder. "All the same, Sheriff. Better not to poke the bear when it's been subdued."

Hieroglyphics flashed in Anubis's eyes, and he holstered his pistol. "The town's yours. There weren't many eligible candidates here anyway."

"Sounds like something a loser would say," Thanatos chimed in.

Anubis removed another piece of straw from his pocket and shoved it between his teeth. "We should do this again sometime, Underworld. When there aren't as many— distractions. And maybe not wait three centuries this time."

"We'll make it four," I snarled, edging my head at the road he'd slithered into town on.

Chuckling into the wind, Anubis turned his back on us, the eerie fog growing denser as it built around him and blanketed his silhouette until it disappeared into darkness.

"Not sure if I should thank you or chastise you for that, old man. That was both brave and incredibly stupid," I told the Sheriff.

He guffawed and rested his rifle on one shoulder. "Please. Those two things go hand-in-hand."

A woman shrieked from a nearby building, tripping over her skirts as she rushed over to us, falling to her knees in front of me. "You have to help me, Boss. Please, you gotta help me."

"Calm down." I held my hand for her to take and hoisted her to her feet. "What's the problem?"

"They took my son. My little boy. He's only four," she screeched, new tears streaking over the already dried tears on her cheeks.

"Who took him?" Thanatos asked, moving to my side.

The woman slapped a hand to her forehead. "The Rattlers."

Not knowing who or what the Tartarus that was, I arched a brow at the Sheriff.

"Oh, they be a mean bunch, boys. Nastiest outlaws you'll run across this side of the west. They're ruthless and don't care if you're a woman or a kid. If they can make money off ya, they will." The Sheriff shook his head and rubbed the woman's back, trying to console her.

A chill fluttered through my bones at the implication—the mere thought of what they could want with a little boy.

"We'll find him, ma'am. I know it's easier said than done, but you stay here and try to keep calm. The last thing he'll want to see when he's back is his mother in hysterics, right?" I squeezed her shoulder.

"Think it has anything to do with a certain Duat god?" Thanatos whispered.

Glaring at the moonlit horizon, I squared my jaw. "No, he wouldn't have had the time."

No. This was something else *entirely*.

TEN
THANATOS

It was a peculiar feeling to have my head in the clouds, my heart warmed, and skin still tingling from my time with Clementine, only to have it all soured by a greedy and self-righteous Egyptian death god. I made no move against him out of respect for Hades, but that didn't mean the urge didn't itch at me every other moment. The art of restraint and control, especially surrounded by so many other gods, became a skill forged over decades of conditioning. It was something Hades himself did and an act we couldn't help each other with, but we had to do it *ourselves*.

With the worried mother begging for our help finding her son, we didn't want to waste any time and planned to set off within the hour while Hades "gathered supplies," and I reassured the townsfolk we'd be back as soon as possible. Their views on us had changed since we'd first arrived—they went from mistrust and loathing to reliance and appreciation of our presence.

Curling her hands with mine, I pressed feather-light kisses against her knuckles. "Please, Clem. We have no idea what we'll be walking into, and I don't want you to risk *more* pain if we're ambushed."

"Alright," Clem succumbed with a frown and pressed her forehead to my hands. "I just don't want to miss one waking moment with you."

"Hey." I squeezed her hands and waited for her eyes to meet mine. "We have an advantage, and you know what I mean, so this shouldn't take very long. It'd be faster if we could openly do things our way, but I'll be back at your side before you can say 'lavender.'"

"Lavender," she exclaimed, mischief glinting in her eyes.

"I should've seen that coming."

Clem clung to my side, fingers walking up my stomach until they reached my chest. "You already have." Her cheeks flushed with pink, and a sultry smile laced with sheepishness played on her lips.

My spine tightened as I dipped into devilish memories of our night together. I pressed my mouth to hers, delivering a ravenous kiss, regretting I'd inevitably need to pull away. I let my thumbs trail the edges of her jaw before stepping back.

"Find that boy, Than, and come straight back to me," Clementine beseeched, one hand idly playing with the poppy charm on her necklace, her gaze harboring a worry that wrung my heart.

"You have my word." After slipping on my brimmed hat, I tipped it at her and slammed my palm into the swinging doors.

Outside, Hades sat on a black horse, a riderless white one complete with a saddle roped next to him.

"A pale horse, brother? Isn't that a bit too—ironic? I'm sure there were other horses." I folded my arms, leveling my gaze on Hades with narrowed eyes.

"You say ironic, I say intimidating. Regardless of how much reputation we've managed to build around these parts, we still need people to fear and respect us." Hades loosened the reins and tossed them to me. "Promise she won't buck you off."

Rolling my eyes, I caught the leather straps and approached the shimmering white horse, its large eyelashes fluttering over its dark orbed eyes. Animals were such keen creatures they could often see through my disguise—sense something off about me and not uncommonly go on the defensive when they realized *what* I was. "Calm down, girl. It ain't your time yet. Promise." I soothed my palm down the mare's snout once her hooves jittered against the ground. After a snort and a light neigh, she relaxed against my touch, nuzzling into my hand.

"Damn. Didn't know you were a horse whisperer," Hades chided, a snarky grin on his face as he leaned on the pommel with arms crossed.

Offering my death brother a scathing glance, I slipped one boot into a stirrup and hoisted myself onto the saddle. "I don't see *why* we need horses." I gestured between us with a quirked brow.

"We won't need them for the whole trip." Hades clicked his heels at the horse's sides and turned it in the opposite direction. "Figured we'd get far enough outside of town, then port halfway to the next safe area then ride the rest of the way. Can't be too careful."

Making my horse trot to Hades's side, I flashed him a lopsided grin. "Admit it. You want an excuse to moon bathe and feel the wind in your hair."

"Would you blame me?" He flicked his wrist at the blanketed black sky littered with glowing white stars. "I could project this on the cave ceiling, and it'd still pale compared to the real thing."

We rode side by side at a steady pace but not a full gallop, edging out of town and to the crossroads with a rickety wooden sign labeling each direction. "How have you done it all these years?"

"Do what? Live underground for most of the year?" Hades

snorted as if the question were ridiculous at this point.

I rubbed the leather rein between two fingers, smooth on one side, coarse on the other. "Not just that. How do you keep it together every time Persephone comes back *smelling* like the sun? *Seeing* her tanned skin? Knowing she soaked it all in for months, and you will *never* have that luxury?"

How long we'd known each other, and I never dared ask, but the situation had begun to shift, and I wanted it planted in his brain.

Hades's jaw tightened, and he removed his hat, hanging it off the pommel. He let out a gravelly sigh and sank back in his saddle. "When Zeus assigned me the Underworld, what choice did I have? It was either accept my fate or be partially at fault for the universe going to shit. With Seph, what choice do I have? I either accept it and make the most of it, or watch *myself* go to shit."

My brother's love life was undoubtedly all his business, but I also knew he and Persephone deserved happiness. He'd fucked up all those ages ago by conspiring with Zeus to kidnap her and make her his Underworld bride, but it *was* ages ago, and he'd since paid his penitence tenfold.

"And you've not once thought about trying to find a loophole? There's always a way around something regarding the dealings of Greek gods, brother." I punched his shoulder.

"Maybe. But I've also been too exhausted to give it much

thought." Hades's eyes formed slits, and he tilted his chin toward Olympus, marveling at the starlight. "Does this *always* remind you of your mother?"

My mother—Nyx. Born of Chaos itself.

"She is the embodiment of the night. Sort of hard to look past that." Snickering, I gave a *tsking* command to the horse, picking up the pace since we slowed.

"You still mad at her?" Hades asked, his tone genuine and fatherly—a timbre I hadn't heard in centuries.

"No. I forgave her a long time ago. Even told her in person. Could I still be a little sore about some of the torture she put me through, calling it 'conditioning'? Sure, but I can't imagine how it felt for a mother to give up her children for *divine* purposes forcibly." Leaning forward, I ran my fingers through the horse's soft mane. "And we don't talk about it."

Hades flicked one rein at my hands—a playful gesture. "You could've done worse for a father. It *could've* been Erebus."

Faking nausea, I covered my mouth. "Don't even put that thought in my head, old man."

We shared a rare chuckle, Hades slapping a hand between my shoulder blades as we reached the first clearing at a safe distance from civilization.

"This should about do it. Don't see horse or wagon tracks here." Hades pointed at the ground, standing straight on his stirrups to do a full sweep.

A twig snapped nearby, and we pivoted in unison toward the sound. A light feminine voice whispered, "Damn."

"Clementine?" I called to the darkness, the sweetness of her tone far too recognizable.

Clem emerged from the shadows, arms wrapped around herself and shivering. "I was really hoping to sneak through when you guys did whatever it is you do to get somewhere fast."

"How did you plan to do that, darlin', if you don't know *what* exactly we do?" Amusement laced Hades's words, his lips forming a half-smile.

"Clem," I started, hopping from my horse to rub her goosebump-littered arms. "I asked you to stay back there. How did you keep up with us on foot?"

Her teeth chattered, and the circles under her eyes looked darker and more profound. "Started on horse and left it at a trough a ways back so y'all wouldn't hear the shoes. I planned on going back for him, of course."

I shared a side-long glance with Hades before settling my gaze back on my lady love. "I asked you to stay back because what we're about to get into is too dangerous. You could get hurt or worse."

"Dangerous? For who? The Greek gods or the already dying woman?" Clem's expression took on an edge I'd never seen until now.

Hades tapped his fingers on the pommel, averting his gaze

elsewhere and not prepared to provide backup.

"I told you back in the saloon, Than. I want every waking moment I can get with you. And if that means a little risk? So be it. You said it: my life's fate is sealed, and it isn't going to be taken away by some outlaw." She stood on the balls of her feet and pressed a light kiss on my chin.

"She has a point," Hades grumbled.

Pointing a stern finger behind me but keeping my eyes on Clementine, I growled back, "I do *not* need your commentary."

Clementine frowned, her chin tilting downward like a scolded kitten.

"Clem, no, don't do that. It's fine. It'll be a little adventure. Just please *stay* hidden. Fated or not. You can still get hurt."

A smile blessed her lips, and she turned her gaze on the horse. "Oh, she's beautiful."

"I'll help you up." I motioned for her to turn around, and wrapped my hands around her waist, hoisting her to sit sidesaddle before settling myself behind her and holding the reins with one hand, my other arm cradled around her.

"Now, Clementine, what we're about to do is referred to by us mythical types as 'porting.' It may feel a bit funny and make you nauseous, but I've been told by some that it made their skin feel delightfully tingly as well." Hades winked at her and slid the hat on his head, ensuring his palm touched his horse lest we risk arriving at our new destination with a mount.

Clementine's head whipped around to stare at me.

Kissing the side of her head, grinning against her skin, I slid my palm to the mare's neck and ported us and the horses to another clearing. We ensured several bushes would serve as extra shielding against surprises, but no sooner had we landed on the dirt, than men yelling and horses neighing blasted from the road.

Hades held a finger to his lips, signaling Clementine to be quiet. Stealthily, we dismounted, and I helped Clem land on the ground without making a sound. We snuck toward the bushes, peeking between the leaves—a Wells Fargo stagecoach. We showed up in the middle of a robbery. Clementine slid her hands over her mouth to stifle the gasp from her throat. One outlaw, fitted with a black handkerchief tied around his mouth, pointed a shotgun in the driver's face, motioning with the barrel for him to exit the coach. The four horses scraped their hooves, neighed, and whinnied.

"Just do as you told, and you ain't gonna get hurt. Hear me?" Black Handkerchief said, shoving the tip of the shotgun to the driver's back to move him away from the wagon and closer to our hiding spot.

Hades caught my gaze and nudged his head toward the outlaw, hooking his thumbs together and fanning his hands like wings. We'd been at this long enough that I knew what he planned and what my part would be. Shrugging off my jacket,

I crouched behind the bush, and gave him a curt nod.

"You, gentleman," Hades started, rising to his feet with a lit cigar, flames already bouncing in his eyes. "Picked the wrong damn stagecoach." Deliberately slow, he moved from the coverage of the bush, puffing on the cigar to let the smoke halfway disguise his face.

The other outlaw, with a stained white handkerchief tied around his jaw, swiveled on his heel, training the pistol on Hades. "Who the fuck do you think you are?"

Hades let out an eerily deep chuckle, giving me the signal with a finger snap. Rising high, making my wings flare from the edges of the bush, but not enough to show my face; I unleashed them, not caring they tore my shirt. Given our positioning, the wings framed Hades, making it seem they were his instead of mine. My non-fiery wings were less conspicuous.

Mr. Black's pistol shook violently, eyes bulging at the menacing sight. "The goddamned Devil. That's what," he yelled, feet shifting backward until his back collided with the wagon.

Shaking his head, Hades hissed. "That asshole is always getting the credit nowadays." He flicked the tip of the cigar, ridding the end of ash. "And I happen to know he prefers to be called *Lucifer*. So—" Hades backed into the shadows, signaling the second stunt of mine for our age-old spectacle.

"—what do you think I elect to be called?"

Hades bowed his head, and I flashed my face through the bushes—death's face—skeletal, macabre, and lifeless. A visage Clementine would *never* see at its fullest.

"Jesus Christ," Mr. White screeched, dropping his pistol and sprinting away, disappearing into the thick woods on the horizon.

Mr. Black remained, still aiming his jittering pistol at Hades, his other palm pressing against the wagon as if it'd protect him.

"Have you suddenly lost the will to live, boy?" Hades asked, sliding from the darkness, eyes still fiery.

"Wh-what?" Mr. Black stuttered, his words muffled from the cloth covering his mouth. "No. No!"

"Then you—" Hades extended an arm, the outlaw pinching his eyes shut and screaming like a child. "—better run." Hades used two fingers, to touch the pistol's barrel and make it glow orange with heat.

Mr. Black didn't open his eyes until the swelter touched the handle, burning him. He yelped and dropped the gun, staring at his reddened palm, then snapping his gaze back to Hades. Hades arched both brows and jabbed his head in the direction the outlaw's partner scurried. A heartbeat later, Mr. Black finally got the idea and ran faster than any mortal I'd seen, tripping several times over rocks and fallen tree limbs.

The driver hugged his hat to his chest, shivering with his

back to a tree and wincing as Hades walked toward him. "Please. Take anything you want. It ain't worth dyin' for."

The flames flickered away from Hades' gaze, and he stopped moving, holding his hands up with palms facing the driver. "I'm not here to rob you in their stead. Just passing through and wanted to stop a misdeed from happening. You're free to continue your route, sir."

"You're not gonna shoot a fireball or some tarnation at me, are ya?" The driver's thick gray mustache bristled.

Hades bit back a smile. "Absolutely not."

"Alright then. Appreciate the help. Whoever you are." The driver slipped his brimmed hat back on his head and tried to keep as much distance between him and Hades as he side-shuffled to the stagecoach. Once seated, he immediately snapped the reins, taking off in a furious gallop, the wagon jostling from the speed.

Taking Clementine's hand, I led her to Hades, who gazed at the stars. Hades glanced at Clementine, frowning when he saw how tired she looked despite the minute grin tugging at her lips. I'd noticed it, too.

"Why don't we make camp for the night and get some shut-eye before the big 'adventure' tomorrow, hm?" Hades placed a hand on Clementine's shoulder, brow furrowed at me.

"Oh, I'm perfectly fine. No sense in slowing us down on account of me." Clementine shook her head, forcing her smile wider, her eyes filled with unavoidable drowsiness.

"Didn't say a word about you, darlin'. I'm beat. Contrary to what most people think, even gods gotta re-fuel their tanks." Hades cupped her cheek with a warm smile before moving into the woods. "We'll find a good spot to make a fire."

He spoke the truth regarding gods still needing rest like any other being. But we needed much less than the average mortal, especially given our ages, and I knew we could still go for days before we'd feel that sluggish pull at our bones. No. He did it for Clementine, and it only upped my respect for him.

Not following them, I held my head low, the inevitable tug toward Clementine's soul growing stronger. And I didn't want to feel it, be *led* by it. Not right now.

"I'll go find us some wood," I announced, pointing in the opposite direction.

The skin on Clem's forehead cinched. "Y'all can't make some, I don't know, appear?"

"Some of us can. But death gods don't exactly deal with plant life and nature." Hades continued to smile at her, motioning for me to leave, that he had it handled.

Clementine let out that infectious laughter. "No, I suppose not."

Hades would keep her safe. He'd protect her in the singular small instance I'd be gone. But I had to distance myself from her, collect my thoughts, and force this wrenching impulse that held power over me away for as long as possible.

Who was I trying to fool?

Hades held fire within his palms through the foliage, using it to warm Clementine until I returned with wood. Grimly, she smiled, and I knew then and there. Shortly after we retrieved the boy—I'd have to guide her home.

ELEVEN
HADES

HOLDING FIRE WITHIN MY palms to warm Clementine and her chattering teeth, I scooted closer, offering a meager smile. "He should be back soon."

"Must be on account of me being sick because it doesn't seem like it's that cold tonight." Clementine wrapped her arms around herself and cleared her throat.

"No need to be strong around me, darlin'. You've earned some rest, I'd say."

Clementine widened her eyes at me, her gaze shifting from the direction Thanatos escaped into the woods and back to me. "Heavens to Besty, how could I've forgotten? You're—*Hades*."

A light chuckle escaped my throat. "That I am. Doesn't

frighten you, does it?"

She gasped and reached forward, wrapping a delicate hand over my forearm. "Goodness, no. Not at all. It's just so easy to forget how normal you two seem."

"Normal. Now there's a word we don't hear often." I kept a pleasant smile to put her at ease.

She recoiled her hand, placing it in her lap, and absently chewed on her lip. "Would you—I mean, could I ask you a question?"

"Ask as many as you'd like." I kept my fire near her and leaned on one knee.

She continued to bite her lip, gaze turning toward the ominous forest. "How hard is this on him? I feel awful."

I blinked, taken aback. "I see now more than ever why Thanatos is so fond of you. Your concern for him, a Greek god *destined* to deal with death, over your own life?"

"Do Greek gods not have emotions the same as humans? Flaws? Weaknesses?" Clementine's knees bounced beneath her skirts, those emerald eyes meeting mine—curiosity and sadness playing in her gaze.

I gave a curt nod. "We do."

"What's yours?" She asked, quick as a whip.

Rolling my shoulders, I cleared my throat and adjusted my seating position. "My flaw?"

Her lips pursed and she nodded solemnly.

"Going straight for the jugular, hm?" I attempted a smile, but when she didn't return it, I let it fade.

"I'm at the weakest point in my entire life, and call me crazy, but hearing the weaknesses of such powerful beings as you are, might give me a bit of strength."

All beings mystical or otherwise had weaknesses. There was no all-powerful entity in the universe who could never be eradicated or represented any form of flawlessness. I wasn't certain it could ever be achieved. To *exist* is to have flaws.

"I'm selfish," I answered, my voice low and distant.

She leaned forward, the fire dancing in my palms casting fractals of orange over her freckled cheeks. "You? How do you figure that?"

"My Queen is doomed to an eternity in the Underworld because I'd seen her picking flowers in a meadow on the surface, thought she was the most beautiful thing I'd ever seen and desired to make her mine. And, with the aid of my brother, I made it so."

Clementine licked her plump lips, eyes casting to the brown grass before floating back to me. "I see. But surely, you've made up for it? So much time has passed."

This would be the first instance I voiced it because I didn't want to admit I knew, but again, she deserved every ounce of extra strength we could offer her.

"We've had many moments of happiness and a lot of sad

ones, yes. But I do have a theory, if she wished to leave, on how she could because she's a goddess." I set my jaw, the flame dousing for the moment I lost concentration.

"And why haven't you told her? To give her that choice?" Clem canted her head to the side, her hand finding my knee again, squeezing it.

Sighing, I scratched my beard. "Because I fear being alone again." I tore the hat from my head, tossing it in the dirt with a scowl. "As I said—selfish."

"Human," Clementine answered with the sweetest smile I'd ever seen grace a woman's lips. "And him?" She turned her gaze toward the woods.

"Thanatos? Imposter syndrome." I focused my gaze on the bouncing flame in my palm.

Clementine quirked her head to one side like she wasn't familiar with the term.

"He doesn't feel he's deserving of success. Of happiness. And it's due to eons of this gods-forsaken job thrust upon us."

"He's so wrong. It makes him all that *more* deserving." Clementine's frown deepened and the flickering flames from my power glinted in her eyes. "Can't imagine the burdens he faces."

"You're helping him though, darlin'. Far more than you know." I squeezed her shoulder reassuringly.

She pursed her lips and nervously rubbed her hands

together. "Is there a heaven?"

The number of times I'd been asked the exact same question the last century, but her asking it bothered me the least.

"Unfortunately, that's not my place to say." A furrow formed in my brow. "But what I *can* tell you, is that you personally won't face nothingness."

Mortification spread her features. "Are you saying some people *do* face nothing at the end of it all?"

Solemnly, I nodded. "Bad people, Clem. Very bad people. And for some, the worst form of torture is eternal darkness."

"That's—that's horrible." She gulped and curled her hands to her chest.

"As I said, these are extremely bad people. But you have the best of hearts, Clementine, and will have a life after this one. Where that is, your heart will guide and the universe will handle the rest."

Clementine chewed her thumbnail, her eyes taking on a certain glitter to them from my words. "Wow. I'm incredibly lucky."

For a woman days away from dying of an incurable disease, I failed to understand the sentiment.

"Lucky?"

"Yeah. How many humans get to know what lies ahead after it's all done? And more—" She sat up straighter, noticing Thanatos emerge from the woods. "—who gets the chance to embrace and love *Death*?"

A remarkable human being. There was no other way to describe her.

"Sorry I took so long," Thanatos huffed, tossing the wood he'd collected to the ground between us. He dropped to his knees to stack it. "What were you two talking about this whole time?"

"Your awkward teenage years." With a half-smile I flashed a wink at Clementine.

Thanatos paused and narrowed his eyes. "You wouldn't."

"Nah. That conversation would last a whole, what? Thirty seconds?" A playful challenge flashed in my gaze.

Thanatos offered a meager snicker and shook his head, situating the wood in a pyramid. Once he stepped back, I tossed my fireball onto the wood, igniting it into a cozy roaring fire.

"There we are. Let's get some rest. At first light we'll head out, find the boy, bring him home, and be back in time for supper, I reckon." Squatting, I lay on my back near the fire, propping my hat over my face.

"Here, Clem," Thanatos said.

Their feet shuffled on the ground, the rustling sounds of a coat being folded following and Clementine cooing a sweet, "Thank you."

We awoke with sunrise, mounting our horses to complete the trek toward the last known location of the Rattlers gang. The trail only led us further and deeper into the woods, various bird calls and critters giving off warning chippers to each other about our presence. The sun blazed through the canopy, making scattered shadows, and the heat had already begun to settle, though it never bothered me.

"We sure this is the right way?" Thanatos asked, his arms curled around Clementine seated in front of him on the white horse.

"Nope. But the townspeople said it was this way and we got nothing else to go off."

A light cough pushed from Clementine's throat. "Well, I'll tell you, if I were up to no good, I'd find me a place in the middle of nowhere to run off to. Think they leave markers to remember how to find the way? Everything looks the same."

"Good possibility," Thanatos answered. "But we also have an—*advantage* over them, if you will."

Clementine gave a light chuckle. "Are you two like hound dogs? Can you sniff 'em out?"

I smiled, remaining quiet and letting the two of them spend as much time together as humanly possible.

"Something like that." A rare snicker floated from Thanatos's throat. "But it's more like a sixth sense than anything else."

A crunching noise caught my attention and I brought us to

a halt, stopping my horse and signaling to Than with a raised fist to follow suit. After a few harrowing moments, scanning our surroundings, a brown rabbit hopped from behind a tree, standing on its hind legs and wiggling its nose at us.

"Good thing we stopped, Hades. That thing looks terrifying," Thanatos mused behind me, making Clementine giggle.

"It's so cute," Clementine cooed.

Shaking my head, I clicked my heels against the horse's sides. "Let's continue on. I feel a heavy presence looming further ahead."

After several more minutes of working our way through the never-ending woodlands, a log cabin appeared within the overlapping leaves and branches. We dismounted our horses so as to not make additional noise and tied them to a tree.

"Please stay here, Clem, alright? And don't show yourself for anything. They can't know you're here," Thanatos whispered, rubbing up and down Clem's arms.

Clementine gave a small nod and crouched behind a bush, making a shushing gesture with a single finger.

Adjusting my hat, I eyed the building's perimeter. Aside from several pairs of footprints scattered in the dirt, there didn't seem to be much activity. "Than, take the rear and I'll go in through the front. Need to catch these bastards by surprise."

"Got it," Than answered, giving a curt nod of affirmation before winding his way toward the back entrance.

I approached the door, my power surging through my bones, ready to unleash a torrential fire storm on anyone inside. Slamming my boot into the door, it swung open to—emptiness. Thanatos barreled through the entry across the room, the curved claws on the arches of his wings peeking from behind his back poised and ready. We arched brows at each other and I made a circling gesture with a finger for us to work the room.

With light feet we each searched in tandem on opposing sides until the faint sound of liquid sloshing in a bottle came from a back room. Pausing in front of the door, I opened it wider than a crack. A man in chaps, red paisley shirt and brown leather jacket sat in a rocking chair swigging back whiskey. Thanatos loomed behind me and together we stormed into the room.

"Where's the boy?" I demanded, making fire ignite in my gaze.

The man shrieked and dropped the bottle, the contents splashing across the wooden floor as the bottom broke, sending shards of green glass in every direction. "Who in the flying fuck are you?"

"Does it matter?" Thanatos stalked toward him, curling his wings from behind his back. "He asked you a question."

The man's bottom lip trembled as he stared at the menacing and lethal black wings arching skyward. "I—"

Making a growl form from my belly, growing louder and

louder as it neared my throat, embers and burnt feathers hovering around me, I held the man's petrified gaze. "Where. Is. The boy. Don't make me ask a third time, you pathetic excuse for a human being."

"The—the—" The man stammered, his hands clinging to the chair's armrests. "—the gang took him. We—we had a buyer looking to adopt a kid. But—but they've been gone an awfully long time."

Thanatos and I shared a concerned side-eye.

"Which direction did they go?" Thanatos asked, his voice booming, making the light fixtures on the walls rattle.

The man winced, sweat soaking his face, and he pointed to his right toward the woods outside. "Listen, I'm just here as a lookout. I ain't had nothing to do with it."

Thanatos stood over the petrified man, pressing his forefinger to the man's forehead. "You're lucky you speak the truth. If I were you—I'd run and never look back at this gang. Don't tempt fate, Howard."

Howard rapidly blinked, staring at Thanatos like he'd recognized him but couldn't pinpoint how or why. After a couple of heartbeats, Howard lurched from his chair and sprinted outside, slipping on the spilled whiskey and catching himself on the doorway.

"Let's head that way. Grab Clementine. We can't leave her here. Keep an eye on her and let me take point." A scowl formed on my features and I nodded to Thanatos after he'd done the same.

After retrieving our horses, we headed into the forest, high noon stifling hot even from the shade of the tree canopy.

"Who steals children only to sell them to other people looking to adopt? I'll never understand the world we live in," Clementine said perched on Thanatos's horse behind me.

"Evil will always exist and has since the dawn of time, Clem. It's an unfortunate balance that separates the righteous from the misled," Thanatos replied.

"Don't fret, Clementine." I looked behind me, tipping my hat at her. "That's why ethereal beings such as ourselves exist—to ensure their afterlife isn't as forgiving."

Clementine's lips thinned, but she nodded in understanding.

"I smell death nearby, Hades." Thanatos's nose twitched before he nudged his head to the left.

"Oh my God. Is it—please tell me it's not the boy," Clem said, her voice cracking, hands cupping her mouth.

"Stay with her. I'll check it out." I turned my horse and no sooner had I brushed through the thicket, a slew of bodies lay haphazard across the grass—bloody and torn to pieces. "Don't come over here, Than. Don't let her see this."

Hopping from the horse, I stepped over the rotting corpses, the humidity in the air causing them to sour already despite being freshly killed. Several wolves emerged from every angle, their mouths stained red along with patches of blood across their chests. Their lips pulled back, snarling, the primal instinct to kill still raging in their veins.

Holding my palms toward them I moved to the center, glaring at them. I'd been given gifts over predatory animals, otherwise Cerberus would've eaten me alive as a pup. I sought out their alpha, taking gentle steps toward him with my hands still on display as non-threatening. The other wolves twitched but didn't retreat as their alpha made no motion. The alpha's bared teeth tentatively disappeared, replaced by a set jaw, chin held high, and a glossy understanding coating his round eyes.

Taking a knee, I reached a hand forward. "You've done your duty, wolf. Time to go home with the pack."

The wolf dipped its head, allowing me to place my hand atop it, and with one yip communicated to its pack, they turned in unison and ran into the forest. Frowning, I scanned the bodies but didn't see one that looked like a small child. An acorn landed on the ground in front of me and I looked skyward, spying a small booted foot slipping back onto a branch above.

"Timmy?" I rose, circling the tree's trunk. "Is that you up there? I'm a friend of your mother's. Come to take you back to her."

One boot hung from the tree limb. "No, you didn't. You're just one of those big mean guys trying to get me to come down."

I couldn't blame the kid for being cautious after an ordeal

like that.

"I have a real nice lady with me. Works at the saloon. Would you prefer to talk to her?" I perked my ear toward the tree when he didn't answer.

"Yes, please," the mousey voice of the boy answered.

Grimacing at the bloodbath surrounding the base of the tree, I waved my hand, camouflaging the bodies so Clem nor the boy saw them. Walking back to Than, I hung a thumb in my belt loop. "Found the boy. He avoided being eaten by wolves by climbing into a tree. Can't say the same for his captors."

Clementine gasped and Than hugged her tighter from behind. "Where's the boy then? Still in the tree?"

"Yeah. He won't come down. Not very trusting toward strange men at present. Don't blame him." I edged my eyes at Clementine, knowing Than should be the one to ask her.

"What if I talked to him?" Clem asked before Thanatos had the chance.

Than caught my gaze and raised a dark brow. "Is it—*safe*?"

"I made sure of it. Come on, this way." I motioned with my hand for them to follow and pointed at the tiny boot hanging from the tree limb above.

Than helped Clementine off the horse and she cleared her throat, tilting her head up. "Hello? My name's Clementine. What's yours?"

The little boot bounced. "Timmy."

156

"Well, hi, Timmy. Do you want to come down from there so we can make proper introductions? I promise these men won't hurt you. They're the good guys." She gave Thanatos a warm smile.

I wouldn't go so far as to say *good*, but we were certainly better than evil.

"Okay," Timmy answered without any more protest.

He shifted onto the limb, curling his short legs around the tree, ready to shimmy down it. His boot slipped halfway down and he began to fall. Clementine shrieked, lurching forward as if she planned to somehow help the boy. Thanatos reached an arm out and caught Timmy with little effort, resting him on his feet a breath later.

The boy stared at Thanatos with widened, questioning eyes, his tiny hands rubbing against one another before he turned to Clementine. He shoved his face in her skirts, trying his best to wrap his arms around her legs, hugging her. Clementine frowned, ruffled Timmy's dirty blonde hair, and caught Thanatos's gaze.

"Why don't you ride the horse with him and I'll follow beside on foot?" Thanatos motioned at the saddle, first helping Clem secure herself, followed by the reluctant boy who grinned once perched on the horse.

Clementine snaked one arm around the boy's middle, using the free hand to hold onto the bridle as Thanatos took the reins and led the horse from the ground. "Than, I feel bad you gotta walk the whole way back. We could switch off at the halfway point?"

Thanatos chuckled and patted Clem's calf. "You know I'll be fine. Just keep making that boy happy until we get him back to his mother. He likes you more than us anyhow."

Despite the wariness pulling at her eyes, Clem gave Than a warm smile and hugged the boy closer to her chest.

"Clem and time, why is the sky blue?" Timmy asked, stumbling over how to pronounce her name and squinting at the cloudless sky above.

Moseying beside them on my midnight horse, I stilled on Thanatos's expression melting at the sight of Clementine with the child in her arms. To deal with the job, a sort of icy edginess had to develop over my heart. But seeing my brother this way, consumed by love and knowing loss—there was no amount of conditioning for that.

"Well, that's a great question, Timmy. You know, I remember reading about this scientist who said that the sun spills all kinds of colors over everything you see, but that blue travels the slowest and that's why we're able to see it." Clementine shielded her eyes with a hand and gazed up.

The little boy giggled. "Colors can't move."

"No? Well, what do you think then?" Clementine tickled Timmy's sides, making him explode in laughter.

Timmy swung his arms up and wide. "I think it's because there's a giant bwooberry that watches over us."

"A better theory than Zeus making the sky match Athena's eyes," I mumbled, managing to pull a tiny wry smile from Thanatos.

Zeus would never admit it, but on rare occasion he'd pay small homages to me and Poseidon and the color of the sky? Was to match Poseidon's dominion—the seas.

"And does this berry have a name?" Clementine asked, biting back a smile.

Timmy squinted one eye and stuck his tongue out the corner of his mouth. "Ted."

"Ted the all-seeing blueberry, hm?" Thanatos asked, nudging Timmy's leg with a knuckle.

The hours passed with Clementine entertaining the boy and discreetly coughing into her handkerchief when she felt the urge, avoiding scaring him with the sight of blood. The further and further we traveled back, Thanatos's jaw tightened and his gaze fell to the ground.

Backing up my horse, I moved to the other side to whisper to him. "I know what's rolling through your head and I'm here to tell you to think of it this way—that boy will never forget her for this. She may not ever raise children of her own but she's made an ever-lasting impact on that boy."

Thanatos arched a dark brow, a scowl distorting his forehead.

"I hate when you're repeatedly right far too many times in a row in a given week."

"I certainly don't." Grinning at him and clapping him on the shoulder, I trotted back to my side to flank the two mortals in our care.

When we made it back to the saloon, Timmy's mother sat at a front table. Her hair was frizzy, the dress unkempt, and the dark bags under her eyes suggested she hadn't slept since we left.

Timmy spied her through the window and jostled on the saddle, Thanatos immediately grabbing onto him so he didn't fall. "Mama," the boy cried out, running to the doors no sooner had his shoes hit the dirt.

A forlorn smile fluttered Clementine's lips and she flicked her fingernails at the reins. "Such a sweet boy considering everything he's been through."

"Don't sell yourself short, sweetheart." Thanatos turned to face her, his hand idly massaging her leg. "Only reason he kept calm was because of you."

Exhaustion settled in her gaze, the slowly dying spurts of her essence calling to me in ways I wished to ignore. "You should take her to her room, Than."

"Yes. I'm very—" Clementine didn't finish and instead slipped from the saddle, falling limp in Thanatos's arms.

Growling and not giving me a second glance, Thanatos

whisked into the saloon. I adjusted my hat and focused on two horse flies mating on a nearby trough, their microscopic wings flapping and buzzing. I felt such pity for myself over the situation I'd put myself in with Persephone and now how selfish it seemed. Because Thanatos would never have a first spat with Clementine, no children, no milestones of any kind. All he'd receive is an end no sooner than had it started and a lifetime to make up for within days.

TWELVE
CLEMENTINE

AS EXHAUSTED AS I was, sleep hadn't come easy the previous night from fear that I wouldn't survive into the next day. Moving became increasingly difficult, and a sort of fog settled over my brain making it challenging to think straight. But when I opened my eyes, Thanatos loomed over me, his chilled hand pressing to my forehead, cooling it. It took several moments for my vision to focus but I knew it was him even through the blur.

"Hold on a little longer for me, Clem." His lips pressed to my temple and soon I was lifted into his arms. "Today, I'm helping you put everything to memory."

Despite me still being in my nightgown, I didn't care. The

thin fabric made it easier to feel the wind against my legs and the sun warming my skin once we reached outside. Thanatos untied the reins of his snow-white horse and lifted me to saddle sideways, holding me steady as he followed and settled behind me.

"Where would you like to go, Clem?" His arms brushed my sides as he held the reins, clicking his spurs against the horse's sides to start a trot.

I nuzzled to his chest, cooing at how taut his muscles felt. "The mountains. A meadow. A nap under a shaded tree. The river where folks are sifting, hoping they strike gold."

A light chuckle rumbled against my back from the death god. "Let's do it all, sweetheart."

He kissed my hair and snapped the reins, leading the horse into a mild gallop.

My senses were more acutely aware than they'd ever been. The faint scents of varying flowers carried in the wind, the unpleasant odor of horse manure, and even the smell of the heat settling in the air.

Tilting my chin, I focused on Thanatos's scent, surprised by the smokey, almost earthy undertones overlapping with cedar and cologne. "No offense intended in the slightest but why do you smell like dirt?"

"You're probably smelling poppies," he whispered against my cheek. "Had you not sensed it until now?"

His question made my chest tighten and I rubbed the poppy charm between two fingers, shaking my head versus voicing my answer. He too stayed quiet and instead, flicked the reins, launching the horse into a full gallop with one hand, the other arm holding me tight. The world zipped past us and I closed my eyes from the jarring up and down motions as the horse's hooves carved into the earth beneath us.

"Clementine," Thanatos breathed a moment later into my ear.

I fluttered my eyes open, realizing I must've fallen asleep from the haziness clouding my brain. "Where are we?"

"A spot that gives you all of what you asked for, Clem." Thanatos lifted me from the saddle, cradling me in his arms again.

A vast mountainside lay in the distance, the sky taking on hues of blue, purples, oranges, and pinks. A large tree with expanding branches, leaves lush with green stood near the edge of a bustling river, the tree's limbs providing ample shade.

"I'd like to walk, if you don't mind. Want to feel the grass between my toes." I offered Thanatos a warm smile, my fingers lazily tangling in his long, dark hair.

Nodding, Thanatos set me down, offering his forearm for support. I leaned on him and took careful steps toward the tree, tears welling in my eyes at the living painting displayed before us. My bottom lip quivered, vision blurring, overwhelmed by the sheer beauty of it.

"Have you ever seen anything so beautiful and breathtaking, Than?" Resting my head on his shoulder, I stared at it, carving it to memory, knowing it's why he brought me here.

"Not in lifetimes," he replied, his breath fluttering the top of my head.

"Can we sit against the tree? Under the shade?"

Thanatos led me to the tree's base, sitting with his back to it and pulling me between his legs. He wrapped his arms around me from behind, holding me tight, and I leaned against him.

"Will I ever see anything like this again, Thanatos? Please be honest with me."

"Yes. I promise you with every ethereal breath I take, yes, you will." His stubbled chin rubbed on my temple and his embrace tensed around me.

Settling against his chest, I let out a wistful sigh, smiling at the sight of a miner sifting in the river further down the bank. "I'm going to ask you something. Is that alright?"

"*Anything* you need, Clem."

I shifted so I could peer up at him, *look* at his expression. "Why do you feel you're undeserving of love?"

His jaw tightened, gaze snapping to the river before slowly returning back to me. "I'm death itself. There's no endearment. No empathy. Just sadness and darkness."

"Oh, Thanatos." I pressed a hand to his cheek. "Death is

a natural part of organic life. Anyone you guide should be thankful it's you. Isn't embracing death, in a way, loving it?"

Thanatos's nostrils flared. "This fate isn't fair to you. It damn-well isn't."

"It may not seem fair, but maybe that's not what it was about. Maybe—" I took his hands in mine, ignoring how icy they felt and running my fingertips between his knuckles. "—my purpose was to allow you to figure out a way to forgive yourself."

He blew out a breath and kissed the back of my hand. "Only to have you torn away from me?"

Grimacing, I sat up, cautiously turning to face him. "There's a lesson there too, god of death. I read a poem once when I was a child, and my favorite part? That it's better to love and lose someone, rather than to have never loved at all."

"You *have* changed me, Clem. I didn't know I was capable of anything beyond giving people pain, consuming their grief, and frightening them." Thanatos leaned in and placed a gentle kiss to my lips. "You've shown me that I can do more."

"Well—" I started, elongating the "e." "—you can be pretty scary when handling bad people. But I find it more attractive than frightening." Despite the tiredness pulling at me, lulling me, I still wanted to see him smile.

The edge of his lips tugged and he gave me just that before running the tip of his thumb under my bottom lip.

"I have to ask. You say your powers only center around

doom and gloom, but death is life. You possess no power over anything, I don't know, living?" I canted my head to the side, catching sight of a trout leaping out of the water from the corner of my eye.

Thanatos rubbed his lips together and hitched a knee, resting his forearm atop it. "The only thing I can think of is this—" He spread his fingers and gray smoky tendrils swirled from his palm, settling over the grass until a patch of red poppies sprouted.

Gasping, I trailed my touch over them, tears building in my eyes again. "My favorite."

"And it's the only flower I can conjure. They're one of my symbols." His callused fingers brushed my collar bones as he took the poppy charm hanging around my neck in his grasp, caressing it, mesmerized by it.

"Thanatos—" I paused, waiting for him to look at me. "I need you to make me a promise." Trailing a single finger down his thin nose, I waited for him to give his full attention.

"I'm listening."

"Don't close your heart to a future love story." I pressed a palm to his cheek.

"Clem—" His gaze fluttered away, and I gently turned his face back to me and interrupted what I knew he was about to protest.

"I know you. And you'll feel you're to blame for me, for this sickness killing me, but I'm asking you to not do that. Keep your heart open. I won't be upset, Thanatos, because I won't *be* here any longer. And I need to know that this kind soul you possess, that—" I crawled onto his lap and pressed our foreheads together. "—someone else will be able to cherish you the way I've gotten to and maybe this one will be forever. But I need you to promise me you won't turn a blind eye."

His hand cupped the back of my head and we both closed our eyes. "I—I don't know if can do that."

"You told me anything I wanted. Didn't you?"

His eyes flew open, those onyx pools sucking me in. "Yes."

"This is something I want. Promise. Me. Make a blood pact or whatever it is that ties gods to their words. I need this, Thanatos." I curled my hands behind his neck, locking onto him.

His jaw flexed and he rolled up his shirt sleeve, revealing the tattoo on his forearm of an inverted sword, poppies, and liquid drops. "I promise you, Clementine Nichols. I won't close myself off to future love if it should cross my path." He dragged his hand over the tattoo and a glowing white poppy appeared in the center, contrasting the red ones. "And this binds me to it."

Taking his face in my hands, I kissed him with every ounce of energy left in me. "Thank you. I love you."

"I love you too."

The colors of sunset began to overtake the sky, spreading an orange glow through the tree's canopy and sparkling gold on the river's surface. The miner had since gone home, losing the natural lighting to see the remnants in his tray. I re-situated myself to lay in Than's arms, readying to watch the sun set for what I knew would be the last time in my mortal life. I wanted to soak it all in with every last breath.

"I'll never forget you. I'll never forget our time together," I said, squeezing his knee.

He went silent, his body tensing beneath mine.

He had to have his reasons, and I wasn't about to pry. Let him deal with it however he needed. I owed him that much.

"I've never seen a sunset this vibrant. Did you put in a good word or something?" I arched a brow at him.

He didn't crack a smile and rubbed my shoulders, staring up at the purple sky bleeding with crimson. "Does it matter if I did?"

"No," I whispered. "It really really doesn't."

"I have a better idea for us to watch the sunset, if you're up for it." Thanatos lifted me from his lap and we stood facing each other.

He unbuttoned his shirt, keeping our gazes locked, his expression solemn. And soon those beautiful raven-like wings sprung from his back. He held out a hand for me to take and I slipped my palm against his with raised brows. "Care to know how it feels to fly?"

THIRTEEN
THANATOS

I'D TAKEN AN INFINITE number of souls from Earth, sending them to Hades for judgment without remorse for any of them. But this? Being at Clementine's side as she lived through her final hours? Pretending I didn't want to scream to Olympus on how hurt I was? I doubt I'd ever experience anything quite as torturous. But every sparkle in her eye, every escaped tear, and every shining smile she gave me made the agony worth it.

I risked someone seeing me with my ebony wings flared, soaring through the skies with a dying woman in my arms. But I didn't give a fuck. I couldn't give her wings as she wished, but I *could* give the illusion my wings were hers as I took her on a flight through the clouds.

Clementine's strength, her will to live, astonished me. But today was it. I'd have to siphon her soul, extract her life, and send it before midnight because today was the day Clementine had to die. And I'd already made the Fates impatient standing ready with her thread pulled taut, *waiting* on me to do my gods-given job. But she earned every spent minute from her vehement resolution.

She lay in my arms, her petite pale fingers winding round and round my long hair. Her eyes had become hooded, and she couldn't decide whether to gaze at my face or the vibrant sky surrounding us. "You're beautiful, Thanatos."

"Thank you." I pressed my lips to her forehead, frowning at how cold her skin felt. "But *you're* the beautiful one."

"Mm, but look at you. Ebony hair being tousled by the wind, those fierce, ethereal wings beating against the air, and don't get me going on that chiseled, handsome face." A weak smile tilted her lips, and she brushed her finger down my chin.

"Sweetheart, what are you doing? You should be looking at this sunset." I forced a light chuckle from my throat and nuzzled my cheek against her head.

"It's a gorgeous view, Than, but this—" She pressed a palm to my chest. "This I want to make sure to put to memory."

And my heart continued to wrench. I promised myself that I'd make Clem's death as painless as possible with my powers. And I knew what had to be done to ensure that the promise continued into the afterlife. She would have to forget me. As if we had never met. Because we'd never be united in life after death like a mortal couple, and I couldn't bear the thought of her missing me for an eternity—heartbroken.

"Take one more look at the sky for *me* then, Clem. The sun is almost gone." I nudged my chin in front of her, and she obliged, smiling and turning her face toward the sun dipping away, a choked gasp pushing from her lips.

"I'm going to miss it here," Clem whispered, her voice cracking like she was on the verge of tears. "Even knowing there's life afterward, I'll *still* miss it."

A vise squeezed my heart now. I tightened my grip and kissed her cheek.

"Is this your mama coming?" Clementine pointed a finger at the sky, nighttime beginning to blanket it, the moon and stars punching their way through.

A small smile managed to sneak onto my lips. "Not exactly. She often disguises herself in the night sky, but when she does, it normally overlooks Greece. Her way of—keeping an eye on it, I suppose."

Clementine closed her eyes and held her arms out to each side, the wind rustling through her hair. "Can you fly faster? Maybe do a barrel roll?"

"Hold onto me tightly, sweetheart," I whispered, my skin warming as her slender arms wrapped around my neck.

With one flap, I poised my wings behind me, sending us into a quick nose dive. Amid the clouds, I spun us in a circle, stopping with Clementine on top. Her eyes, despite their tiredness, lit up. Lazily, I fluttered the wings, allowing us to glide through the air in an embrace. Flipping us back around, I flew faster, pumping my wings through the air enough to make our hair flail behind us, some of hers tickling my face.

Clementine laughed, and her eyes closed with contentment before the chuckling became coughing and sputtering. Instantly, I halted in the air, frowning at her blood-speckled lips. "You should probably take me home, Than. This—thank you for this. It was lovely."

Giving a solemn nod because words escaped me, I flew us back to where I'd tied off the horse and, after disguising my wings, made the melancholy trek back to the saloon. I carried her to the stairs with a dozen pairs of eyes looking mournfully onward, the patrons removing their hats as I passed, knowing what was coming to poor Clementine. As best as she tried to hide it, the past days had grown far more apparent. I took each step ascending to her room as if I waded through caramel. My jaw clenched as I stood in front of her door, unable to find the will to push it open.

"Hey," Clementine's weak voice said, her hand lifting to my face. "It's okay. I'm ready, Than."

And now, here she was, trying to comfort *me*.

"You don't have to be strong for me. It's more than okay *not* to be ready, Clementine. I'd even understand if you hated me."

The word kicked the air from my lungs, but I'd let her feel any way she needed to make it through this, to *do* whatever she needed to do.

"I've told you before. You're my guide, Than. This sickness killed me. Not you. I could never hate you." She sat up, still draped in my arms, and winced, her other hand finding my face. "And I *am* ready. I've lived as best of life as possible with the time given. I'd go so far as to say I'm not scared anymore."

Nodding, I brushed a feather-light kiss against her lips. "Time to go home." Gently pressing my shoulder against the door, I walked her inside, shutting it behind us.

She tugged my shirt sleeve. "Can you put me down a minute? I—I don't want to pass on in a nightgown." A delicate smile edged her lips.

"Do you need help?" Resting her feet on the floor, I held her hands to ensure her steadiness.

"I'll manage." She squeezed my hands before turning for the bathroom, holding onto the wall for balance. "Do I have a few minutes?"

Clenching my fists at my sides, I gave an earnest nod, and she slipped into the bathroom, the faint light of a single lit candle bouncing from the bottom crack. My deathly skeletal form had forced itself out on my right arm, the fiery cracks in the blackened bone sizzling amidst the silence in the room. I slid that arm behind me so as not to frighten her. Once the death-god form took over, I could do little to mask it until the soul it called for was claimed.

It enraged me that my instincts still thought of her as just another soul—another mortal on their journey to the afterlife, and I'd be the one to send them. No. She was more than that. And I refused to let any impulse attempt to dissuade me from thinking anything less. She wasn't any other mortal, she'd been *my* mortal. My sweet Clementine. A scowl overtook my features, hardening my face to stone, my fists shaking at my sides.

The door creaked open, and I softened my expression, still keeping the skeletal arm hidden from view. Clementine stepped out in an eggplant dress with black lace, her hands smoothing out the front.

"I bought this for such an occasion. Not sure how it works, but if I need to be stuck in one set of clothes for the rest of my afterlife, I wanted it to be *this* dress." She ran her hands over and over a wrinkle that refused to flatten out. "Just wish I could've gotten all the wrinkles out before—"

I appeared before her, the wings flaring and stretching to their entire span. Taking her shaky hand in mine, I ran my thumb over her knuckles. "You look beautiful. Wrinkle or not."

Her emerald gaze lifted to my wings, eyes glistening with building tears. "Thank you—" A cough interrupted her. "—

thank you kindly."

"Come lay down, Clem." I rested a hand on her lower back, guiding her.

She sat on the bed's edge before scooting back. I helped her lift her legs the rest of the way and held my hand behind her head as she slowly lowered to the pillows. "I'm so glad I had the chance to meet you, Thanatos. Greek god or not. You were what kept me going, kept me smiling."

"I'll be eternally grateful to whatever entity decided to put you in my path, sweetheart. Eternally. Grateful." I smoothed a hand through her hair, calming her.

She reached for my hand and squeezed it, holding it in her grasp. "I've never liked goodbyes, so instead, I'm going to say, 'Catch you later, cowboy.'" She laughed, tears streaking her cheeks now, and another bout of coughing followed.

"Catch you later, sweet Clementine," I responded, using every ounce of strength I had to keep the anger and fear swirling through me buried deep. "Do you remember the butterfly I showed you before?"

She nodded.

"I want you to focus on it. Count how many veins you see in its wings. How many times does it flap them? Can you do that for me?" I made the blue butterfly appear on my shoulder, a mirage I'd used infinite times to help ease innocent and fragile mortals.

She nodded again, her eyes already fixated on the insect. After letting out a deep, disgruntled sigh, I lifted the skeletal hand, which possessed death's touch, and placed it on her cheek, slowly lowering my mouth to hers.

"I promise I'll never forget you. And I promise to keep as open of heart as I can." I pressed my lips to hers, giving one last kiss before turning it into…something else.

Opening my mouth, I lifted my head, coaxing her mouth to stay open as the blue swirling tendrils of her spirit flowed into me. Clementine's eyes never faltered from the butterfly, and it kept her from seeing my face turning skeletal the more of her soul I siphoned. I rubbed the back of her neck, the veins in her temples starting to protrude, her eyelashes flickering. But she'd feel no pain, no recollection of any of it. Because not only would I take her soul but also any memories she had of me.

The hand she had tightly pressed to mine slowly loosened its grip until it lay flat on the bed, her eyelids fluttering shut. And as I took her final breath, she went boneless in my grasp, her vibrance extinguished. Shuddering, I snapped my mouth shut, already despising myself for what I'd done—what I *had* to do. Lifting her, I pressed her back to my chest, holding her in my lap and moving the hair from her face.

A single black tear rolled down my cheek. I caught it once it reached my chin to keep it from falling and staining her dress. And I sat there with her in my arms for what seemed an eternity, selfishly begging the universe to send her to the Fields so I might watch over her until the cosmos no longer existed.

FOURTEEN
HADES

I'D BEEN IN THE saloon when Thanatos whisked Clementine up the stairs but didn't say a word. I could do very little to ease my brother's pain and hatred for the universe. Nothing I said would lessen the blow, and telling someone you're "sorry" when you weren't at fault nor could you do anything to change one godsdamned thing seemed—superfluous.

I didn't envy what he'd endure in that upstairs room and what he'd deal with for years afterward. And I should only feel so fortunate as to know despite the current status of my relationship with Persephone, there was little chance I'd ever have to hold a dying spring goddess in my arms. The thought alone caused a seething pain to tighten in my chest. The night continued without so much as a whisper of indecency—the townsfolks' unspoken way of honoring Clementine's memory. She'd been a shining light amidst her brethren, and without her, no doubt the city would lose a bit of its splendor.

I took the opportunity to soak in the moon and stars, a sight foreign to the likes of the Underworld—a cavern of perpetual darkness where fire and brimstone served as its only light. Such brilliance lay in a blanket of stardust and distant planets. I stayed near the saloon but stepped outside, leaning on a post to stare at the sky until something needed my attention, but the people didn't require my services. Probably just as well. Clementine deserved the calmness, and serenity to pass into the afterlife. And Thanatos deserved the time undisturbed with her.

Sitting on the stoop outside the saloon, I rested my forearms on my knees, readying to watch my last sunrise for nearly another year. The sun peeked over the horizon, splurging a line of vibrant crimson—that split moment was my favorite part. It only happened for a nanosecond before the colors splashed into orange and yellow. I closed my eyes, contently sighing at the warmth fanning my cheeks. Shrugging off my coat, I rested it beside me and rolled up my shirt sleeves, willing the sun to kiss every bit of skin I could offer.

"Last day, ain't it?" The Sheriff asked, his body blocking the sun.

Subduing a growl from the interruption, I opened one eye with a dimpled grin before rising, my height allowing the sun to greet me again. "Yeah. But I'll stick around until dusk if it's all the same to you."

"Shit, stay as long as you want, Boss. Might want to go check out the Mutton farm, though. It's on the outskirts of town?" The Sheriff chewed on a piece of grass, his liver-spot-ridden hand raising to point behind me.

"That so? Any reason?" I readjusted my sleeves.

"Been losing cattle. Some they found dead. Others have disappeared without a trace." He spit at the ground before continuing. "Know it ain't your usual fare, but that's their livelihood. They lose a few more cows, and they're gonna have a rough time making it through the winter."

"I'll check it out before I leave. No big deal." After giving a curt nod, I flipped the hat back to my head and slid on the jacket.

The Sheriff nodded solemnly. "Damn shame about Clementine, hm? Such a sweet gal didn't deserve an end like that."

"She'll be missed. Unfortunately, the universe works in mysterious ways." I bowed my head to him before walking past.

And ways that deities themselves couldn't fully understand.

Walking to the two horses tied up across the road, I frowned at the sight of Thanatos's white one I'd rented as a joke. It seemed terrible form now. Electing to ride to the farm, devoid of any magic use, I hoisted myself into the saddle and paused, peering up at Clementine's window. Than hadn't left the saloon all night, and today, he'd have to bury her. I did *not* envy him. Clipping my spurs at the horse's sides, I took us into a steady gallop, avoiding the shady parts of the road and purposely letting the sun roast me.

All of this happening with Thanatos and Clementine had my mind reeling regarding my relationship. And I knew I procrastinated going back for good reason. We needed to talk. It was a conversation I'd been avoiding for years, but I owed it to both of us to have it. I would make it work if she wished and figure out a way to let her go if she didn't. Simple as that—or so I hoped.

Releasing a hefty sigh, I paused at the view of the humble farm in the distance. It wasn't the largest in the state by any means, but a decent enough size, it'd cost a pretty penny to keep running. Slowly, I made my way to the fence, stopping in front of it out of courtesy and respect waiting for one of the owners to spot me.

A middle-aged man with graying straw-like long hair and a floppy brown hat emerged from behind a plow. "Boss? Pardon me saying, but what in the Sam Hill are you doing out this way?"

"Heard you were having a cattle problem?" I leaned on the

saddle.

The man took his hat off, scratching his sweating head as he walked closer. "I am, but I wouldn't expect to bother you with such a small matter. I mean, you're—you."

"Nothing is too small, friend. I'm always here to help, and less cattle means less income for you and your family." Holding out a hand to him, we shook. "Mind telling me about it? Take me to the spots where you found the dead ones?"

"Well, thank you. Follow me." He motioned with his hand, and I followed him to the pasture. "We found two of our cows dead in the pasture within a couple weeks of each other. And two calves have gone missing."

I hopped off the horse, discreetly using my power to scan the cows, noting the brand mark on their hinds. "When do you brand them, exactly?"

"Not until the calves have been weaned." The farmer raised a thick brow. "Why?"

Thanks to my godly intuition, this would be easy to solve. Was it wrong of me to hope it'd take longer to stretch out my last day?

"Is it possible they stole the calves to put their own brand on them and killed the mothers so they couldn't come back?" I scratched the stubble on my chin. "And your brand wouldn't be there if they were accused of stealing?"

The farmer's jaw dropped, and he threw his hands to his

hips. "That is entirely plausible. And makes a whole hell of lotta sense."

"Let me take a look around. See if I can't find any—" No sooner had the words begun to leave my mouth than the herd started excitedly mooing, driving our attention to the cows.

A man with a bandana covering his face used a prod on a calf's ass, forcing it toward the gate, its mother hoofing the ground and shaking its head.

"Assholes getting so desperate they aren't even bothering to try this shit at night?" The farmer spat before waving his arm in the air. "Hey you, get the hell off my property," he bellowed, alerting the thief, who slammed the gate shut and made a beeline for his awaiting horse.

I'd have preferred him not to alert the thief to my presence, but here we were.

"You'll get your cows back. I guarantee it. Just give me a few." Giving the farmer a wink, I whisked onto my horse, snapping the reins to chase after the thief.

Discreetly, I made a rope appear in my free hand, leading the horse into a full gallop. Leaning back, I wound the lasso through my hands, readying it. The thief hunched forward, snapping the reins with extra enthusiasm, and looked behind him every other second. I tossed the rope in my palm, eyeing my shot, fire burning adrenaline through my veins. My horse drew closer, and I threw the lasso, securing it around the thief's chest. He launched from his saddle after one tug, landing on the ground in a violent thud. As I slowed my horse, I purposely let him drag over the rock-ridden ground several feet before stopping.

"I believe you've taken something that isn't yours. Isn't that right?" I wound the rope around my forearm, holding it taut.

The thief clambered to his knees, whimpering. "No idea what you're talking about."

"Wrong answer." I clicked my heels to the horse's sides, making it jolt forward and drag him through the mud.

The man yelped, and the bandana disappeared, torn away by a jagged branch, slashing his face.

Stopping the horse, I pulled the rope, causing the thief to land on his belly. "Care to try again?"

Defensively, the man held up his hands, gulping. "Alright, alright, yeah. I stole a couple of cows."

"You say this so casually. As if it's not a crime?"

The thief ran his shirt sleeve over the sweat and blood caking his forehead. "I wasn't gonna take no more. Honest to God's truth."

Glaring at him, I read into his soul. The mortal had never done another deed. This was his first offense. "Why did you do it in the first place?"

"My family. Most of our cows came down with this disease. Damn near killed the whole herd. I—" He pressed his hands together in prayer. "I didn't want them to starve."

Solemnly, I nodded, loosening the lasso but pointing a stern finger in his face. "I can respect that, but you shouldn't do it at the expense of putting *another* family in danger."

There'd been no point in bursting flames in my gaze or making the ember wings peek. At the heart of it, he had a good soul and acted out of desperation. And dare I say in these final moments on the surface I felt—sympathetic?

"You're right. You're absolutely right. And I won't do it again." The man stayed on his knees, lips twitching as he stared at me.

"You're going to give two cows to the farmer you stole four from. The calves will have to stay where they are, but you want to make up for misdeeds—"

Ah what the Tartarus…

I snapped my fingers, igniting a flame, his eyes darting to my hand. "—You give what you take."

"I—yes, yes, of course," the man stammered, launching to his feet and shaking, his hands still pressed together as if worshiping me. "Consider it done."

When he made no motion to move, I lit a fire in my eyes—only a little. "You best be on your way with that."

He did a hitch-step, sprinting after his freely roaming horse. "Buttercup," he shouted, using two fingers to whistle for it.

The last task I performed on the surface this season *had* to be a righteous mortal hoping to provide for his family. It was enough to give me an ethereal headache.

I returned to the saloon to make a final visit and mark my words with all the townsfolk. Standing in the foyer, I raised a finger, a tiny bit of fire wrapping around it as I spoke. "You all be good while I'm gone. Remember. Just because I'm not here doesn't mean I don't have eyes and ears around every corner. And I *will* hear about it and *will* address it next season. Understand?"

Everyone gave silent nods, respectfully resting their drinks on the table to provide me with their full attention. After slipping on my hat and tipping it at them, I pushed through the swinging doors with a deep sigh. Time to return to my kingdom of the dead. But before going home, one final stop—visiting Thanatos at Clementine's grave. I would offer any form of consoling Thanatos felt akin to taking, even if it were as simple as standing beside him in silence.

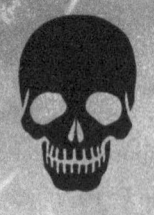

FIFTEEN
THANATOS

IT WAS A QUAINT headstone but one that suited her humility. She wouldn't have wanted anything more and probably would've requested something even simpler than what I chose—curved stone with a poppy flower etched within a circle at the top, filigree bordering, and in the center her name, dates of birth, death, and the words: Cherished and Loved. A fresh pile of dirt lay over her grave, and I knelt beside the headstone, my arm draping, forehead resting just above my wrist.

"I had them bury you under the shade of a tree facing the mountains, Clem." The words muffled against my shirt sleeve. "You seemed to enjoy that view during our last day together, and I know you won't remember it, so here it is."

Lifting my head, I let out a long sigh and brushed my hand over the top of the headstone, ridding it of dust still hanging from the carving. The grass surrounding the tombstone was lush and green but still not vibrant enough to match her radiance. Fanning my palm, I made clusters of red poppy flowers grow, and they'd stay there for eternity—never withering, never dying.

"I'd say I'm sorry brother but I know what little worth the word holds," Hades said behind me.

I couldn't bring myself to look at him at first. I didn't want him to see the genuine pain and weakness plaguing my face. And there was no need for apologies. Even as king, he has no power over death-condemned mortals.

"What you can do for me, Hades—" I started, still facing Clem's grave. "—is to tell me *where*."

Hades slipped a hand over my shoulder, squeezing it. "Rest assured, she's in the Fields."

A relief I'd never experienced whooshed from my lungs, and I let my eyes fall shut.

"Did you plan to visit her?" Hades squatted beside me and pushed his fingertips together, both our gazes focused on the headstone.

Gingerly, I let my fingertips graze the poppy petals. "I hoped to watch over her. And now I can, but I siphoned her memories of us."

Hades made a light whistling sound. "That must've been difficult. But I understand why."

"I promised her as painless as possible." I tightened my jaw. Pushing to my feet, I raked a hand through my hair, desperate to change the subject. "Aren't you due back?"

Hades bunched his pants in his palms before standing and sighing. "Yes. I'm stalling because I don't know what version of Seph I'll be getting."

"Whichever it is, you should consider bringing up what we discussed, brother."

A yellow songbird flew from an above tree limb, flapping its tiny wings and diving, landing on Clem's tombstone. It canted its head from left to right and sang in chirps and warbles. A small smile managed to edge its way onto my lips.

"I wish there's something we could've done, Thanatos." Hades clapped a hand on my shoulder. "But remember, Clementine wasn't the end."

"No." Curtly, I shook my head, meeting my Underworld king's gaze. "She was the beginning."

Hades gave a reassuring squeeze to my arm before letting out a gruff sigh. "Rest assured, she's already settled in the Fields. I asked Persephone to make her a priority."

"Thank you," I whispered, closing my eyes as a rare wind rustled the trees in the dank summer heat.

After Hades took glanced around us, he splayed his hand

at the ground. "Seems as good a place as any, and quite frankly, I'm at the 'don't give a shit stage' of my visit." A stairwell leading to the Underworld formed in the dirt, the opening glowing a fiery orange, embers floating through the sky in spurts.

"I'll report in within the next day or so." I lifted my chin, delving back into honorable duty.

Hades slipped the hat from his head and combed a hand through his hair. "No rush. Heal, Thanatos. Not sure you know how much you'll need it."

Nodding once to my king, I remained silent. He descended the stairs, and once his head disappeared within the opening, the hole sealed shut, leaving behind smoky vapors that the wind carried away.

What was I to do with myself now? Mortals didn't cease dying when Death itself had reason to grieve.

"Well, well," a familiar voice said behind me in a sing-song tone. "Word in the clouds is you managed to get laid finally."

Dionysus had *no* clue about the fire he played with, and today, I didn't care to explain.

Turning on one heel with fire blazing in my veins, I came face to face with the god of wine and frenzy. He'd been smiling, but the amusement faded when his gaze landed on my stony expression, his dark beard drooping with his lips.

"Than?" Dionysus hesitantly asked, taking a step back.

Without responding, I sprung the black wings from my back, the deadly talons whistling.

Dionysus pointed a finger and retreated further. "Thanatos, what the Tartarus? You know I'm only sh—"

I cut his words short, using my wings to propel me forward, and bunched his cream linen shirt in my grasp. "Today *wasn't* the day, Dion." The words flew from my throat in anguished rasps and snarls.

Methodically, Dion slid his arms to mine, and, with one swipe, shoved them away. "Alright, Death. You need to let off some steam? Work something out of your system?" He skirted backward and rolled up his shirt sleeves. "Fine. But I ain't making it easy." His long dark hair streaked with sun-bleached tendrils hung over his bronzed face as he widened his stance.

If it were any other day, I may have retorted with a witty comeback, but I didn't feel like talking. I wanted to *destroy*.

I arched my wings, talons poised to attack, feathers curving and rustling. Dionysus glared at the claws, his arm extending, a thyrsus appearing in his grasp—a speared weapon forged of a fennel-stem scepter, wound with ivy, its tip a razor-sharp pine cone. He spun it around and beckoned me with his hand.

Death's touch flashed down my right arm, making the blackened bone with fiery cracks appear, and I lurched at him with a mighty flap of my wings. Aiming one talon at him, he deflected it with his spear. I countered with an uppercut of my skeletal hand, landing on his chin and sending him flying into a tree. The spear clambered to the ground, bouncing, and I paced a square in the grass, waiting for him to get to his feet.

"You planning on telling me what the fuck is wrong with you, Thanatos? Or are you content to bruise me first?" Using his boot, he scooped the spear and hoisted it upward to his awaiting hand.

Still saying nothing, I slashed one talon at him, then the other, my wings curling and unfurling to accommodate the swift motions. They hadn't seen combat like this—ethereal combat—in decades. The moves felt stiff on my back at first, but with every swing, they loosened like conditioning muscles.

I pointed a rigid arm at the grave before soaring high above, coming down in a lethal aerial strike I had to barrel roll out of once Dion raised his spear.

Dion's hands squeezed the spear's handle. "A grave? No offense, brother but, don't you deal with them on a daily basis? Why—"

Fanning my wings wide, I wafted them, sending a splurge of air, toppling Dion back on his heels. Speeding forward, I batted the spear away like a pesky gnat and gripped his shirt—this time much *tighter*. "It was *her*."

"You mean the? You and her—oh. *Oh.*" Dion dropped the spear, displaying his palms at me open and non-threatening. "Sorry. I—"

I slammed my fists against his chest, throwing him against a tree trunk and cracking its bark.

"Than, I get it. I do. Loving a mortal, let alone losing one so young is never easy."

Growling, I bared my canines and curled my wing talons at his throat. "Do *not* talk about Clem as if she were just one of my lost playthings."

Dion's mouth curled downward, his eyes unflinching at the sharp claws nearing his neck. "That's not what I meant. I know you're hurting. Do what you need to do."

Guilt, remorse, confusion, and hurt coursed through me like an uncontrollable cancer eating at my insides. Releasing him, I blinked and tumbled away, my wings drooping at my sides. There'd been no predicting the anguish Clem's death would invoke in me, the unfamiliar sting burning in my eyes, or the seeming hole in my heart that left me breathless. A continued battle between making the world burn for taking Clem away from me or secluding myself to darkness for the rest of eternity throttled through me.

"What do you need to do?" Dionysus stood still, a wrinkle of concern distorting his forehead.

"My job," I replied, my shoulders hunching forward, hair falling in an onyx waterfall around my face as I lowered my chin.

Dion folded his arms, dipping his head to try and look me in the eye. "Your job? That's the last thing you should be doing. Even gods need to grieve, Thanatos. And don't try and tell me Hades hasn't already suggested the same damn thing."

Lifting my chin, I let the deathly skeletal form take over half my face, my gaze darkening to thunderous clouds.

Dionysus leaned back, the skin beneath one eye twitching. "Or—maybe you need to do your job. A distraction?"

Without bidding him any formal goodbye, I folded my wings behind me, my brain going into a fog, and my body acting of its own accord. Smoke curled at my feet, swirling around my legs and hips until it engulfed me, and I ported away, not knowing where I intended to go, just anywhere but here. Nowhere remotely close.

I appeared on the apex of a giant emerald hill, hundreds more of them rolling in grassy waves as far as the eye could see. A stone castle rested on the highest hill in the distance. Gray clouds littered the sky, a light rainy mist coating the air. A cow mooing nearby had me disguising the wings, making them disappear.

Slowly peering over one shoulder, the cow grazed on grass, its jaw rotating in continued circles, staring at me. An older man in a plaid tweed flat cap appeared over the hill, yelling something to the animal in a language I'd scarcely heard before. Gaelic, perhaps?

The man stopped dead when his gaze fell on me with widened green eyes matching the surrounding grass. He spoke again, and it unnerved me that, despite my power, I couldn't understand a word he said.

"Do you speak English?"

The man removed his cap and quizzically scratched his bald head. "Course I do. What are you doing out here in the middle of nowhere, mucker?"

I inhaled deeply, the scents of rain, barley, and soil calming my nerves. "Where is this?"

The man lifted one half of his upper lip skyward, tilting his head back so far I could see the gray hairs sprouting from his nose. "Are you codding me?"

Speaking the same language and yet still lost in translation. I looked at him blankly.

The man slapped his cap against his thigh, a hoot of laughter barking from his chest. "Ireland."

SIXTEEN
HADES

I'D APPEARED IN CERBERUS'S cave before anywhere else, knowing his greeting would undoubtedly surpass any Persephone would have for me. He didn't disappoint. No sooner had he smelled my presence than three pairs of crimson eyes appeared from the shadows. His sizeable form, resembling a skyscraper, sprinted for me, all four legs sliding across the moist stone ground, attempting not to tackle straight into me.

Laughing, thankful for the bubbly feeling swelling in my chest, I got one of his three heads in my arms. His large pink tongue lapped my cheek, slathering drool on my beard and hair. Grimacing, I ruffled his ears. "Missed you too, buddy."

I nuzzled into his neck, the fur's softness lulling me into a daze. The faint scents of narcissus and lilies floated in the air, Cerberus's body stiffening beneath my grasp. "My Queen," I hummed, keeping my eyes shut, cheek still pressed to the dog's chest.

"What gave me away? Cerberus?" Persephone's voice, once so fragile and wistful, had taken on an edge in the past years. But it suited her now—commanding and powerful.

Edging a smile, I pushed away and patted Cerberus's head. "Your scent, Seph. Always your scent."

"Did you—have a good time?" She stood tall with her hands folded behind her back, eyes searching my face, a sort of nervous jitter to her that I couldn't place.

After scratching under all three of Cerberus's chins, I walked toward Persephone with a raised brow. "As much as one could condemning mortals. You alright? You seem—antsy."

An innocence shimmered over her features, her eyes going doe-like. "I'm fine. Perfectly fine. I just—" She moved her hands in front of her, fingernails picking at each other.

Still squinting at her, I moved closer, reaching a hand to rest on her trembling ones. "Seph, you know you can tell me anything. What is it?"

Her lips thinned, and those pale eyes lifted to meet mine. "I—I missed you."

Those three words should've made a triumphant symphony strike warmth in my heart, but instead, all I could focus on was how her lip twitched when she said it. A quirk I'd come to learn when she *lied*.

Either she hid something or decided to try and make things work.

Bringing her knuckles to my lips, I pressed a soft kiss there. "I, uh, missed you too."

"You did?" Her eyes made three fluttery blinks. "I didn't mean to ask that."

I couldn't recall another time she acted the same way, except for when I spied Cerberus with one red claw and questioned her about it. She fibbed at first, claiming she had no idea what I spoke of, and confessed weeks later she had gotten bored and painted the dog's nails with Olympus knows what. Apparently, she forgot one when she removed the coloring to prevent me from ever finding out.

"I wouldn't blame you for being skeptical. We haven't said it to each other in what seems like a decade." I traced a finger up and down the inside of her forearm.

She tensed under my touch, her throat bobbing.

Tartarus. She *definitely* hid something. But what stung worse? I didn't honestly care.

"Come here, Seph," I opened my arms to her, waiting for her limbs to wrap my torso.

She pursed her lips and leaped at me, hugging me so tight she was almost convincing. "Oh, Smoky." The nickname she gave me when we were at our happiest and rarely ever said now.

After inhaling of her sweet fragrance, I traced a hand through her wheaten locks and pressed my cheek to her temple. "Walk with me in the Fields. I want to check on someone."

Persephone peeled back, curiosity playing in her gaze. "That woman you asked me not to delay with?"

It was subtle, but a tinge of jealousy echoed in her tone.

"Yes." I held my hand out for her to take and interlaced our fingers before porting us to the glittery entrance for the Elysian Fields. "Thanatos. He—" My brother's pained face, the ever-lasting hurt plaguing his eyes—the thought itself made my insides ache. "—he loved her."

"Thanatos," she whispered with remorse and an ounce of relief.

As we strode hand-in-hand over the green pastures and perfectly manicured stony paths of the Fields, no soul would sense our presence unless we wished. Everyone dressed the way they wanted, did what they desired, and experienced their chosen weather. Some mortals preferred the snow over perpetual sunlight. But I knew precisely where Clementine would be.

"That had to be difficult for him." Persephone squeezed my hand.

I brushed my thumb against her palm. "You have no idea. I'm unsure how he'll bounce back after it. But he always finds a way."

Persephone squatted and plucked a white rose from a bush littered with them, positioning it within her hair. "I fear he'll do something drastic."

"Oh? Like what?" I paused and turned her to face me.

She brushed lint from my shoulder. "I'm not sure, but knowing him, he's blaming himself and will feel the need to be punished for some ungodly reason."

And here I thought I knew the god of death well.

Cupping her cheek, I caught her gaze with mine. "I'll talk with him when he's ready. Right now, I know he needs his space."

"Understandable." Persephone scanned the area, her interest piqued. "Do you know where she'd be?"

A brunette sat beneath a wide willow tree overlooking the riverbank. There wasn't a doubt in my mind. It was her. I pointed, and together, Persephone and I walked over to Clementine, invisible to her. She sat with her knees at her chest, arms wrapped around her legs in a deep purple dress. A contented smile played over her lips as she watched the occasional trout jump from the bubbling waters.

Persephone placed a hand over her chest, her eyes closing, and she let out a plaintive sigh. "I've never sensed a purer soul than hers. What's her name?"

"Clementine," I answered, my voice cracking.

Persephone's eyes danced open, and she chewed on her bottom lip. "And she loved him back?"

I wrapped an arm around my wife's shoulders, hugging her to my side. "Until her dying breath."

"With such light against Thanatos's darkness, she clearly was put in his path for a reason." Persephone curled her hands under her chin, gaze never faltering from Clementine. "I thought I was the light for you once. Springtime brought to the darkest depths of the universe."

A scowl edged my features, and gently, I gripped her shoulder and turned her toward me. "Persephone, you've always been that for me. Nothing's changed in that regard."

Her lips took on a lamblike curve. "Yes, they have. I'm not the same goddess you saw picking flowers in the meadow. Some of that light, it's been—doused."

Agitation pulled tight across my forehead, and I pulled Persephone against me, porting us to our royal bedroom, and held her hands. "I need to ask you something, Seph. And I need you to be honest with me. Can you do that?"

Reservation danced in her eyes, but she squeezed my hands. "Sure."

"Are you happy?"

It seemed so frivolous to ask, but we hadn't discussed it. Ever. And why should we spend the rest of our eternal days heartbroken and feeling alone when we weren't?

She gaped at me, silently at first, before spinning away and giving me her back. "Hades," she whispered, clapping a hand over her eyes.

That action told me all I feared was true, but I needed to hear her *say* it.

Stepping behind her, I trailed my fingers over her lower back, her skin only centimeters from my touch through the thin pink dress fabric. "Tell me."

Her gaze dropped to her sandaled feet. "Sometimes I am."

My stomach became overlapping knots in all forms of disarray. She said the words we feared to say to the other, but they stung no less.

"Only sometimes? Shouldn't we strive to be happy more times than not?"

She tugged my shirt sleeve, the rose she placed in her hair earlier dropping from it, and I pushed it back with a single finger. "No couple is happy *all* the time."

"Persephone," I beckoned, leaning in to place a chaste kiss on her lips.

She traced a finger over her mouth, her eyes glassy as she peered at me. "Yes?"

Unease racked my brain, and my throat suddenly grew coarser than the Sahara. "Have you heard of a shade?"

"A shade? Should I have?" Persephone cocked her head to one side like a bewildered kitten.

Releasing a haggard breath, I rested my hand on her nape. "It's a god's version of a soul."

Her lips parted, and the expression in her gaze suggested the wheels of her mind turned. "A soul? Why are you telling me this?"

I bent forward and kissed her forehead. "Nothing you need to worry about now, but just promise me you'll remember I mentioned it."

A squeak escaped her throat, and she rested her head under my chin. "Alright, Hades."

Massaging between her shoulder blades, I spoke into her hair, "What do you wish to do, my Queen? Before I have to return to my duties in Tartarus?"

"Will you lay with me?" She tilted her head skyward, gleaming at me. "I just want to be held."

"Of course, Seph." I pressed a quick peck at the corner of her brow and stepped back, holding out an awaiting hand. "But first, I have something for you."

Her eyes lit up—bright and innocent. "Oh? A present?"

"Yes," I whispered, half-smiling. Digging into my pocket, I produced the wooden narcissus flower I carved for her, sparking my magic into it and making it glow a glittering yellow forever. "I made this for you."

Persephone's lips parted as she took the trinket, tears welling in her eyes. The shimmering magic reflected in her eyes—

eyes full of wonder, appreciation, and happiness. My heart thudded against my ribcage. I hadn't seen that expression in so long I scarcely remembered how boy-like it made me feel.

"Hades, it's beautiful." She raised to her toes and placed a sweet kiss against my cheek. "Thank you."

She slipped her hand in mine and let me lead us to the vast bed covered in black satin and silk. Peeling back the covers, I lay on my side, spreading my arms wide to welcome her to me. Tears filled her eyes, and she stood at the bed's edge, gazing down at me before leaning in and kissing me. She slowly pulled away and cupped my cheek, a doleful smile curving her lips. I softened my eyes as she crawled in front of me, giving me her back and nuzzling against me. She curled the wooden flower to her chest, holding it there as if someone would miraculously show up to steal it from her. With a strained sigh, I wrapped my arms around her and simply held her, just as she desired.

I'd planted the seed for a solution I know she would've never considered because most gods had no idea the decision they had with their shade. In a way, it allowed most of us to be in more than one place—a presence in both. And until she came to her own conclusions, I'd wait for the day she grew the courage to leave the Underworld—to leave *me*. And whether it be weeks or a hundred years from now, when the day came, it wouldn't be any easier to bear.

SEVENTEEN
THANATOS

I COULDN'T HAVE WOUND up in a better place to wallow in self-pity. The view was majestic, with rolling green meadows and the Irish Sea in the distance. Mortals were scarce if you didn't count the occasional wandering cow. And there were plenty of abandoned castles to escape to the shadows within. I continued to do my job but never let them see me in any capacity, nor did I dare look them in the eye. I'd done everything in my power to ensure Clementine experienced no fear as she passed, and I had little strength left to give another mortal the same courtesy yet. The terror in a human's eyes when they knew the time had come was one I'd grown accustomed to but never enjoyed seeing. And until the sting of

Clemetine's absence faded into a dull ache, I couldn't stomach the sight of it.

While amidst mortals, I spent most of my time in disguise, observing them. From talks on the street, this country had outlaws not unlike those in the American West, but organized and strategic about crimes they committed—some form of mob, they called it. Something I intended to keep in the back of mind for future use and safekeeping. Time would undoubtedly heal the many wounds carved into my skin and guts, but it may have been time I wasn't willing to wait. The past days, I cycled my options, only to come up blank at every turn, and knew the singular thing I could do to make it somewhat tolerable—an atonement.

And that's why I found myself standing on the dark sands of the river Styx, waiting for Hades to return to his throne. He'd undoubtedly argue with me about my decision but honor my request and choices. I respected him for caring enough to attempt to talk me out of it, knowing there'd be no swaying me once I'd made up my mind.

Several heartbeats later, the King of the Underworld appeared, slinking onto his throne, his face in his hand. Whatever troubled him seemed enough to cause him not to notice me.

I cleared my throat and lifted my chin once his gaze cut to mine.

"Thanatos? What are you doing here?" Hades stepped down from his throne, closing the distance between us and clapping me on the shoulder.

Folding my arms, I tightened my jaw. "I've come to ask for a favor, brother."

"Oh?" Hades's light brows lifted. "What would you ask of me?"

Stepping forward and broadening my shoulders, I lifted my chin higher. "I need you to *curse* me."

His brow raised higher, and he lifted the hand resting on my shoulder. "Persephone was right thinking you'd want to punish yourself over this."

Shaking my head, I kept my expression stony. "Not a punishment. A means to keep a promise."

Hades rubbed his chin, his gaze falling to the coarse sand brushing our feet. "And if I agreed to this, what exactly are you suggesting?"

The macabre image of Clementine's eyes falling shut, her body going eerily still in my arms, limbs limp at her sides, plagued me.

"Only those tied to our world will see my true face." I pointed at myself. "*This* face."

The skin between Hades's eyes twitched. "And what would everyone else see?"

I carved the memory of Clementine's shimmering smile in

my mind. "However, they choose to see death. Truly see it."

Hades raked a hand through his white hair. "You realize that means the people in our town would probably be terrified of you?"

Terrified of me as they saw nothing but a skeleton or rotting corpse upon looking at me.

"I think it's about time we find other pastures to roam anyway. It's been years. We took care of Anubis, and they seem sorted."

And with Clementine gone, there was nothing left for me except pained memories around every turn and lurking in every hallway.

Hades slid his hands behind his back and slowly nodded. "And where do you intend to call home, then?"

"I'm considering Ireland."

"Beautiful country." Hades smoothed a hand down his robes, stalling.

Stepping closer to him, I squeezed both of his shoulders. "Brother, will you do this for me?"

A profound sigh escaped Hades's lungs, and he lifted a single finger, placing it on my forehead. "I curse you, Thanatos. Whenever a mortal lays their eyes on you, if they bear no connection to our world, they will not see your true face but how they view death."

A sharp sting surged up my spine, settling in the back of

my skull. Holding my head, I stumbled backward, a static-like shock buzzing over my skin. But it wasn't enough. I swirled my hands around myself, making a tattered black cloak appear on my form. Securing the hood over my skull, I tilted my chin downward, disguising myself further within it.

"I fear one day you'll resent me for this." Hades flittered his hand around the vast cave. "For all of this."

What did one say to their brother, superior, and friend when you couldn't tell them something would never happen?

"Perhaps. But not today, Hades. Or tomorrow."

Hades gave a solemn nod. "Don't make yourself scarce all of a sudden. And I'll make it an order if I have to."

Letting my right hand fall to my side, I didn't try to suppress the death hand from showing itself. Flesh disappeared, replaced with the blackened bone and molten cracks. "I'll visit again soon."

We had no need to exchange more words now that Hades did my bidding and I disappeared from the Underworld in a plume of smoke. I stood in an abandoned bedroom within one of the older castles I found in Ireland, staring at my cloaked form in a dingy mirror. For whatever reason, the sight of my bronzed skin irritated me, and I made it turn as pale as a ghost. And those eyes gleaming back at me in the mirror bore no meaning behind them any longer. With a wave of my palm, darkness overtook my gaze, replacing the humanized dark brown eyes given to me by my mother.

"May my skin pale like a corpse and my gaze fog until I feel worthy of *life* again."

THE END

Catch the first book in the Contemporary Mythos series:

The King of the Underworld may have found a woman truly capable of melting his cold, dark heart.

HADES (Contemporary Mythos, #1)
BUY IT ON AMAZON

STAY TUNED!
WWW.CARLYSPADE.COM

ACKNOWLEDGEMENTS

FOR ANY LOYAL READERS of mine who took this journey with me: Thank you. I know this particular story wasn't my usual "happily ever after" fare, but it felt needed for whatever reason. The concept of one's mortality (unless you're a Greek god) is never a comfortable conversation, and most choose not to think about it or brush it aside. The idea of being present on this planet only to be gone at any given moment has always made me uneasy. Did I do enough to leave even the tiniest of ever-lasting impressions? Did I waste away my years? Did I leave too many loose ends from neglect or stubbornness? And so, as much as Clementine served as a stepping stone for Thanatos, she also helped me through a mental block.

To AK, who continues to be my knightess in shining armor, hunkering down to get me feedback in time to publish, thank you again from the bottom of my heart. You never fail to say what needs to be said, and I'll be forever grateful for your polite candidness.

And to the new readers who are just finding my work and this was your first introduction to me: I'll be blunt in saying most anything else you experience of mine will be much more light-hearted, romantic, and swoony. But sometimes, as a writer, you need to step out of your comfort zone and explore.

To everyone, hug your loved ones, check in on your friends, and, for lack of a better phrase, don't ever fail to stop and smell the roses.

ABOUT THE AUTHOR

CARLY SPADE is an adult romance writer who has been writing since she could pick up a pencil. After the insanity of obtaining a bachelor's and master's degree in cybersecurity, creating worlds to escape to still ate at her very soul. She started writing FanFiction (which can still be found if you scour the internet), and soon felt the need to get her original ideas on paper. And so the adventure began.

She lives in Colorado with her husband and two fur babies, and revels in an enemies to lovers trope with a slow burn.

Find her online:

WWW.CARLYSPADE.COM

```
Printed in the USA
CPSIA information can be obtained
at www.ICGtesting.com
JSHW030854200923
48668JS00005B/47
```

9 798986 999333